Hypsipyle
and the
Curse of Lemnos

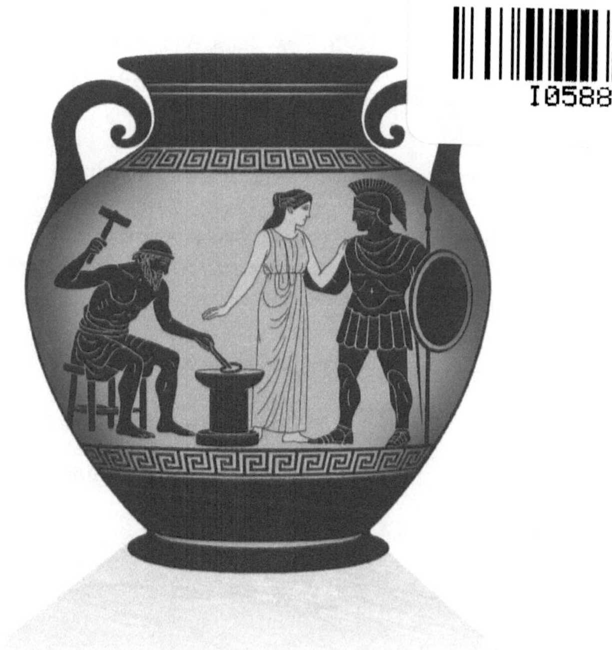

A novella by

KAREN MARTIN

WOMEN UNVEILED SERIES

HIPSIPYLE AND THE CURSE OF LEMNOS

This is a work of fiction drawing from the ancient Greek myth of Hypsipyle.
Names, characters, places, and incidents either are the product of
the author's imagination or are used fictitiously.

First published in Australia in October 2025 by KazJoyPress (Australia)
Cover design and layout by Working Type Studio

Editor: Jane Ormond
www.kazjoypress.com

BISAC: FIC010000 FICTION/ Fairy Tales, Folk Tales, Legends & Mythology
ISBN 978-0-6451922-9-2 (paperback)
ISBN 978-1-7636685-0-8 (ebook)

National Library of Australia

A catalogue record for this
work is available from the
National Library of Australia

Υψιπύλη

pronounced Ip-sip-i-li

HELIOS

From his position high above the mortal veil, the Sun God gazed down upon the world with sight that pierced cloud, shadow, and pretence. The chariot of Helios had not yet dipped beneath the curve of the horizon when an incandescent glint caused him to pause.

Through delicate veils of Aphrodite's private chamber, he spied the God of War decorating her illuminous nakedness with a golden necklace. The sheen of jewellery sparkled like a secret.

Helios squinted for a better look. "Ares," he verified, "bold as ever."

He tilted his radiant head. "And Aphrodite." He licked his lips with unrequited desire for this most wondrous Goddess. His loins ached. His lust to remain forever fanciful, for the Goddess of Love was beyond his reach. Why should Ares be so lucky? Why indeed?

*

Hephaestus wiped salt from his brow, all moisture having evaporated. It would not do to have pieces of immortality drop into the small metal arrow being beaten out. Or would it? He set aside his hammer to pick up tongs and turn the shaft. Heat drank from his underarms leaving a residue scent of salt, earth and last night's raki. The blaze inside his workshop sizzled and sucked out the air, leaving a glow of white-hot charcoal. He licked his dry lips and tasted the effort of his labour. His hog breath huffed an inner foulness devoid of humour. The trauma of being scorned by his mother Hera remained as a permanent scowl. Tool in hand, he struck again, the rhythmic clang of hammer on anvil defiling any silence.

Hephaestus, aware of Helios at the threshold, ignored the visiting god and continued his task. Sparks showered and molten metal hissed around him. When finished, he paused and stood upright. His muscled back twitched.

"You've come to blister your feet or brighten my shadows?" Hephaestus asked.

Helios smirked. "I come with truth," he said. "And apologies for being the messenger of ill tidings."

Intrigued, Hephaestus appraised his visitor with a raised eyebrow.

"Aphrodite," Helios said, "lies with Ares. Not once. Not in passing. Often."

The forge fell silent save for the rasp of cooling metal. Hephaestus snarled. "You know this to be true?"

Helios raised his eyebrow. "Do you forget who charts the sky? I am the guardian of oaths and an all-seeing witness, my friend. I come to advise you of an oath betrayed."

Hephaestus grimaced from the weight of treachery. "So, the God of War thinks he can trespass into my wife's boudoir."

"And she welcomes him," reminded Helios.

Hephaestus scratched his head. His obsidian eyes gleamed with purpose. "Thank you," he grunted. "I will give them cause to burn."

Helios smiled, "I am on hand to help. Let me know when." He left to pasture his steeds and ride the golden boat back east and prepare for the new day. Of reckoning, he hoped.

Hephaestus grabbed his hammer and began pounding the

metal arrow-head. His anger raised bile from his liver, competing with the putrid arena of his mouth. He thirsted. For revenge. For retribution. He fed the fire more fuel. It would take many hours to lessen his rage of Aphrodite's unfaithfulness. Hours spent devising a plan.

THE LOVERS

Two gigantic wooden doors opened into the spacious bedroom chamber. Three large arched windows drew the eye to the garden outside despite the light descending into a hushed lilac twilight. Helios had passed some time ago and wisps of cloud supplied a canvas for his pastel setting.

Ares walked across the polished marble tiles and gazed out to the panorama of hills and valleys spread below. Ringlets of jasmine curled across the external stone wall, kissing the air with sweet fragrance. He turned and smiled with satisfaction at the pink, white, and red rose petals adorning his bed, adding their subtle perfume of promised love to the room. The scents mingled and swirled in a delicate dalliance with a shy breeze. Ares inhaled with anticipation.

"Alectryon," he called, summoning a young soldier into the room. Alectryon unbuckled the God of War's breastplate and with devoted reverence placed it on a stand. He left the room and returned bearing a tray heavy with bread, olives and succulent fruits. Another tray bore a flask of wine and goblets.

"Remain outside and wake me before Helios rises," Ares commanded as he poured the wine. A swish of silk sweeping across the tiles announced his lover's arrival. Turning slowly, he drank in her beauty. Shimmering and magnificent. She walked to the windows, her glorious body silhouetted in the evening's waning light. The purple and white weave of her robes clung in adoration to her toned and voluptuous form. Her golden hair cascaded in waves down her back. A simple tiara of interlaced jewels and minute dainty blooms graced her head, complementary to the necklace adorning her neck. Finding satisfaction with the scenery laid out before her, she turned to face Ares. Her eyes brimmed with desire as she approached him.

Ares' gulped. Rising juices filled his mouth. To distract himself, he handed her a goblet. "To my Goddess." He raised his cup and slugged it down in a mouthful, before tossing it aside to sweep Aphrodite into his arms. An intoxicating aroma of sensuality filled the room and, surrendering to passion, pleasure became their conversation.

*

Helios did not tarry. A trap had been laid, and he trembled with anticipation, eager to attest to its outcome. Beaming through the open arched windows, he spied the lovers still entangled in bedsheets. He grinned. Grabbing a passing movement of air, he sent it swirling down to Hephaestus. Swelling with importance, the movement became a draft and delivered its message in moments. Hephaestus responded with a snarl. Descending to the bowels of his furnace, he took up his enormous bellows and, with the strength and determination of a cuckold god, pumped the air with fervour.

Expanding and contracting, he directed the force of air to Ares' chamber. As the silent pressure entered through the window, a hidden metal mechanism clicked and released an intricate, translucent netting laid in secret upon the bed. This exquisite web, woven by Arachne, snared the lovers within.

Hephaestus ploughed the air. Contracting his bellows, he maintained pressure. With enormous strength, Hephaestus extracted the netting, and scooping Ares and Aphrodite in its fine threads, carried it by his fury to the top of Mount Olympus. Whereupon the net foundered and both God and Goddess tumbled out, splayed naked onto the ground. The other gods, at Hephaestus invitation, had gathered with curiosity and witnessed the bizarre spectacle of their degradation.

Ares leapt to his feet and roared. Pride and dignity had long departed, and his eyes scorched with rage. He helped Aphrodite to her feet. Surrounded by raucous laughter and taunts, she suffered their insults with quiet disdain. Seething she looked up at Ares. "This is his disgrace. His abasement shall not go unanswered. Revenge is mine."

Wrapping the bed sheet around her to deny any onlooker the pleasure of her intimate beauty, Aphrodite stormed away to her chamber to consider her next move. The grass below her bare feet softened, bending to avail themselves to her stride.

As the other gods left and their jeers receded, Ares returned to his chamber to find Alectryon still asleep at the door. The vision of his sleeping guard blazed fury through his veins and with livid words cursed the young man, transforming him into a rooster. "You are tasked forever to announce the rising of Helios," Ares screamed.

THE CURSE

Aphrodite simmered alone in her bed chamber. She dismissed her attendants, who fled, desperate to hide their amusement from their mistress. She paced the marble tiles, fuming at Hephaestus' disrespect. She paused in front of a gilded framed mirror and tossed back her mane of thick curls. She surveyed her image. How glorious. Even the thunder in her eyes looked becoming. She addressed the image as though it were her husband.

"You are an oaf and a hypocrite. You petition Zeus to return my bride price. Bah. You are a fool." Her eyes glowered as she watched herself pretending to confront him. "Answer me from your height of moral duplicity. How many children have you sired with that sea nymph Cabeiro? You think I do not know?" Snorting, she flung accusations at the mirror. "Three sons and, I believe, as many daughters. All hobbled with your ugliness."

Aphrodite swung away and paced the length of the room. "I have one lover," she seethed, "and you behave as a child. I require a god for my needs, not some clumsy pathetic smithy. Tend to your fire, for it is the only heat you are capable of producing."

Her conversation tapered away at the sound of the doors to her chamber opening. Ares strode in. "Zeus be dammed for this immortality shit!" she shouted at him. "I want to kill him. I want him dead and buried and ugh, gone." Aphrodite flushed, anger and frustration competing to grace her cheeks. Ares thought she had never looked so radiant, and he swept her up into his arms. Their bodies entwined, calming her temper.

"What to do?" Her question hung in the air.

Ares reined in his passion and set her down. His finger stroked the outline of her cheekbone. His casual remark belied its power. "Immortality being the case, consider where Hephaestus is most vulnerable. Where you can strike to hurt."

Aphrodite withdrew from his touch to adjust her robes. Goddess of Love, what would she know about tactics of war? A slow smile uncurled like a whispered conspiracy. She knew where his heart lay. "Hephaestus loves his island more than anything," she replied.

"You do know there are goddesses that relish the act of revenge. Perhaps seek their wisdom?"

Aphrodite beamed at her beloved God of War. Of course he would have a battle plan. The twinkle in his eye confirmed her answer. "The Erinyes," she grinned, awed by the enormous potential. Known in foreign lands as the Furies, these gracious goddesses of vengeance could devise a splendid solution. It helped knowing that their justice lacked pity. She cupped Ares' face in her hands and kissed his nose. "Brilliant idea, my charming strategist. Perfect. He wants war, I'll give him war." She left before Ares could reap his reward.

*

More ancient than the Olympian deities, the Erinyes resided in Erebus. While the descent did not thrill Aphrodite, the prospect of revenge spurred her onward. She passed several low altars and pits at the entrance of temples lining the paved road, and observed worshippers chanting with their palms facing downward, gesturing toward the earth. Black or dark-hided animals burned in sacrifice, offered to some chthonic god who inhabited the Underworld. She did not pause to discover who. She preferred her worship to be incense-scented with libations of honey and wine. All this doom and gloom was depressing.

Reaching her destination, Aphrodite drew her veil over her head and covered her nose. The pungent stench of death and decay loitered too close. The Erebus formed the final passage for souls journeying to the Underworld. Despair and dejection saturated the air. Morbidity hung heavy in corners, feeding mould that clung to anything that stayed still for too long.

She hesitated before sitting down on the bank of the wailing river Cocytus to wait for the Erinyes to arrive. This rueful stream carried the laments of the dead, a cacophony of whinging, denouncing and bemoaning. 'No wonder the goddesses are feral,' thought Aphrodite, 'if their task is to hear the complaints of these pitiful mortals.' Despite the abject misery, it provided an apt meeting place, for further upstream, Cocytus formed a lake known for being the home of traitors and treacherous beings. Hephaestus would have been in good company. She spat.

A screech heralded the arrival of Tisiphone, a harbinger of destruction and malevolence. A flurry blurred the space between them as a crowd of phantoms stumbled out of her way. Tisiphone stood glaring at the Goddess of Love.

Tisiphone's head seethed with writhing serpents, their slither and hissing harmonising with the shifting sounds of the dead surrounding her. Her skin was mottled grey with corruption and suffused with venom. Shrouded in black with her sunken eyes narrowed in disgust, she pointed her funeral torch at the illuminous goddess.

Aphrodite stood to greet her. "My dearest sister of the dark," she began. "We, who share the blood of our father Uranus castrated by Cronus," she paused, "I know it's been a while but I come bearing witness to the infidelity of a brute husband, who violates our marriage oath and has humiliated me. I seek your wisdom for vengeful ruin."

Hate drooled from Tisiphone's lips. She tasted Aphrodite's wrath and shivered in a spasm of inspired cruelty. The throng of snakes entangled in her hair sensed a rise of sadistic spite pulse through Tisiphone's body and jolted erect in gleeful anticipation of a strike. She opened her mouth and released a fiery vapour that carried a heartless, cold-blooded sound, curdling the space. Aphrodite surmised it was laughter.

Tisiphone threw back her head and shrieked, summoning her two sisters, Megaera and Alecto. Aphrodite felt the chill of their arrival. The dim surroundings could not hide their monstrous forms draped in black. Aphrodite heard rumour they bore wings, but she could not see them so assumed they may have been cloaked. Each sister also possessed a headful of venomous squirming snakes.

Aphrodite sensed the eyes of Megaera upon her. Shrunken into hollow cheekbones, blood dribbled from them, dripping onto the ground. Megaera's domain stretched over those who transgressed moral bounds through betrayal and deceit, and in her role as avenger of infidelity, she stood as the ordained hand of retribution. Megaera spoke in a powerful, snide tone.

"We are daughters of Nyx, born of blood that fell from deception. Sworn to shadow the breakers of oaths, the defilers of bonds, the liars who smile. Where promises rot, we rise. Where vows are broken, we walk unbidden. No breach escapes us, no guilt fades beneath time's dust. We do not forget. We do not forgive. You, sister Aphrodite, Goddess of love and longing wronged by the forger of shackles, mocked by marriage forged in fire, we hear your call upon vengeance. We who speak for the dead and scream for the dishonoured, will take your grievance and fashion it into punishment. By oath, by blood, by divine decree, justice will be done."

Aphrodite smiled. She enjoyed the dramatics. These chthonic deities knew how to put on a good show. They embodied the fabric of ancient tales, showing how the pursuit of justice could manifest in both divine and terrifying forms.

The triumvirate huddled close to negotiate an appropriate penalty. Hephaestus would not get off lightly, for while Alecto took delight in cursing people with endless anger, Tisiphone revelled in vindictive destruction, and Megaera focused her wrath on matters of broken trust.

The Erinyes sniggered, proud of their creation. They stood and faced Aphrodite to proclaim victory. "You want blood? We'll give you a massacre." In a twisted weave of their individual traits, the sanction of their curse swallowed up the air and held time silent. As they spoke, the power of their chant rose in sprinkled flakes of ash to be dispersed upon the island of Lemnos.

"Let the hearts of Lemnos' men turn cold to their wives, and their eyes stray to the Thracian captives. May desire twist their souls from hearth and home. And when love's fire burns for the foreign, may wrath bloom in the hearts of Lemnian women. Let them rise as one with knives in hand and ash in hearts, and slaughter those who scorned them."

As the Erinyes dissipated into the darkness, their mocking jeer caused a wave of weeping to follow in their wake. Their words echoed through the corridors of the underworld: "The women from Hephaestus' beloved Isle will do what you cannot."

Aphrodite rubbed her slender fingers together and shrugged. 'And so it is done.'

*

And so it was done. The women of Lemnos when spurned by their husbands in favor of the Thracian women, were so enraged by neglect and infidelity, planned a revenge inherited by proxy.

HYPSIPYLE AND THOAS

"Let us walk, Patér."

Hypsipyle traced the lines of her father's face with an affectionate gaze. When had he grown so old? As a child, she cherished the times he replaced his crown with his old straw hat to stroll the garden with her. Thoas took her hand. His tenderness rattled her. She sniffed with abrupt purpose to stave off a swell of emotion and inhaled an aroma of surrounding blooms. She sunk into their perfume hoping to be soothed. Their distraction lasted long enough for a wave of childhood memories to wash through her. But as delightful the moment, her recall failed to shake off her gloom. This would be their last walk.

Unbeknownst, as father and daughter they escaped Aphrodite's cruel revenge. It were the husbands who were targeted, epitomising Hephaestus' own sexual infidelities. But all men of Lemnos would share the same fate. The women were united in this decision.

Something felt unjust that her father should die along with the husbands. But Hypsipyle could not name it. Walking in silence next to him, she relived the secret meetings, when the women met and reached their unanimous decision. All men. King Thoas would not be spared.

*

The women gathered in a quiet twilight. A sea mist enveloped them as they sat close, shoulder to shoulder, skirts damp from the ground. The meeting evolved through necessity, all summoned by an inner wound. For some time, conversations in kitchens, on streets, and at the market all begun with a descending hopelessness: *'I don't know what to do.'* Words uttered by every woman, until the priestess Iphinoe approached Princess Hypsipyle. "We need to talk," she said. And so the women gathered. Uncomfortable, confused, annoyed.

The hushed silence spread toward the dark horizon. Pollyx, once nurse to Hypsipyle, and respected as a wise village elder, stood up and walked into the centre of their circle and addressed the women.

"When did your husband last touch you?" she asked. "Or looked at you? Called your name?" A murmur. A shuffling of bodies. A tightening of shawls. Some women hung their heads. Young women, new to the marriage bed or budding with child, stifled sobs. The floor opened:

"They look at the Thracian girls like they're goddesses. But we're treated like dirt beneath their feet."

"They bring them gifts, while we who raise their children eat broth made from bones."

"They stink of other women, of oil and perfume. I asked my husband if he'd laid with another woman and he laughed in my face."

"They eat our food. They wear our linen. But their hearts are gone. We are ghosts in our own homes."

As the women shared their stories, awareness emerged. The men had abandoned each and every one. No woman escaped their rejection. Rage threaded its way between them like a creeping vine.

"It's in the soil now," said Alkippe, another village elder. "Like weeds. Their behaviour has crept into the root of things."

Hypsipyle turned toward her. "What do you mean?"

"The scorn," Alkippe replied. "The turning away of eyes that once saw us. The stench of their concubines. It festers, and turns to rot."

Hypsipyle closed her eyes. Alkippe's words resonated, replaying a lesson learned from her mother, Myrina. Memory beckoned. Her beloved mother, dead from the time of Hypsipyle's threshold to maidenhood, had shaped the gardens of Lemnos. She had taught Hypsipyle, 'When weeds overrun the olive grove, you set the field alight before the rot sets in. You cleanse the field with fire'. Hypsipyle shuddered.

Iphinoe spoke up, calling for calm and to bring the stories back to the circle. Tales of the women's experiences filled the night. Quiet and deliberate, Iphinoe proclaimed, "something has taken them."

A woman called out. "Lust." Another joined her. "Cowardice." "Weakness," cried another.

"I think it is something else," said Iphinoe. "I feel a texture of something, but it is difficult to speak of, to convey its essence. It is slippery to the senses. Almost not there, its very presence is hidden." She paused, desperate to articulate. "It is hidden in black, in dark, in the shadow. And it has turned their hearts to stone."

A collective gasp, a stunned silence. Looking around, a sea of wide eyes scanned each other for confirmation. A curse? No one dared say the word out loud. Hypsipyle took the lead. "Are you suggesting we, or them, are cursed?"

Pollyx interrupted, "Or maybe this is what they have always been like, and we have refused to see it?" Tension snatched the breath of all. Were they always like this? The question cut deeper than blame.

"Curse or not, they are not our men anymore. And we are not

their women." A chorus of voices agreed.

"Then what are we?" asked one woman.

"Free," answered Pollyx.

Her answer created a strange, bright and terrifying mood within the group.

"What to do?" asked Alkippe. "If we do nothing, if we let this rot grow, it will choke everything. Our daughters. Our future. The men have turned their backs. What can we do?"

"What do free women do with those who treat them like nothing?" Pollyx asked. "To those who disrespect, abuse, deny?"

"We burn the weeds," said Hypsipyle. "It is better to scorch the field than let the weeds take root."

Some women nodded while others, understanding the stakes, stared into the fire, jaws clenched.

"Then let us cleanse what cannot be healed," murmured one.

Pollyx reached over and took Hypsipyle's hand. "We need to plan," she said. "We will not strike like Furies in the night. We will be patient. We will decide, together."

The women met again three moons later, this time in Aphrodite's temple beyond the wind's prying gusts. The moon, hanging low and swollen, cast a pale eerie light. It too, excluded from the conversation. This was women's business. Mortal women's work.

Hypsipyle stood in the centre of the gathering. No crown or cloak. One sister among many. A sister to those whose beds had gone cold, who pined for the men lost.

"They have slept beside us," she began. "They trust our hands. Our silence. Our stillness. They will not expect the food we serve."

"It must be the same night," said Pollyx. "All at once. Otherwise it will turn to chaos and blood in the streets."

"There's no room for fear," said Alkippe. "No wavering."

Hypsipyle turned to Aethra, a student of the renowned healer Hygeia. "Can you provide us a brew that will bring a deep sleep?"

Aethra considered the request, then answered, "I can make a concoction steeped with valerian root, hyoscyamu, and the sleep's eye flower. A small dose will mellow the body. A larger one," she hesitated, "is stronger."

"We will serve this draught in their food," said Hypsipyle, "on the night of the new moon. When the world is darkest and the gods look away. All those agree?"

The unanimous verdict reverberated loud and strong.

"We wait," Alkippe said. "Until they are heavy with slumber. Then we use blades."

"We have agreed all men, but what of the boys?" The woman's voice squeaked tight and reluctant.

"Spare the children," said Hypsipyle. "Aethra, can you prepare a sleeping draught to protect their innocence?"

Soft weeping exposed both fear and sorrow. "Those who cannot bear to do it," said Pollyx, "may leave the door unlatched. Another will do what must be done." They left in the silence of final decisions, hugging each other with love and courage.

*

No-one mentioned the plan again, but every glance and shy smile confirmed their commitment. Tonight, the night of the new moon, they would administer retribution to the men who betrayed them.

"Patér, in this last month have you noticed anything amiss?"

Thoas nodded. "It's as if all you women are on your monthly bleed together. Emotions seem high, the air fraught with tension. It reminds me of the eve before going into battle. I feel this daughter, but I lack understanding to interpret. Can you offer insight?"

Hypsipyle ignored the misogynist overtone of his answer and spoke her concern. "The women, we, wonder if some curse has been laid. It is my opinion that it is the men who are behaving irrationally. Many, if not most, have wandered from the hearth or summoned Thracian women to replace their wives in the marriage bed. They break their oath without fearing any consequence."

"Many?" Thoas chuckled at her reply. "I would agree, Hypsipyle, that some may have strayed. But this is not new. Even Hephaestus, husband of the Goddess of Love herself, sated his itinerant desires. Men must sow their seed. They respond to an innate desire that if their wives cannot or will not satisfy, will see them find distraction elsewhere. This is not a curse, but man's behaviour. Come, dear daughter, let us enjoy our walk and remove such madness from our conversation."

She responded with a slight nod of compliance. But her thoughts refused to retreat, instead sustained her frustration.

"Yes, let us walk," as if her words could put them on a path leading to a different future. Determined to savour their time together, she withdrew into a familiar comfortable silence that often accompanied them. Thoas hummed under his breath, his hands clasped behind his back. "You always rushed ahead on this path when you were small. You called the olive grove a forest, remember?"

"I remember." She knew the story that would follow.

"One tree, the most beautiful, grew from a pit your mother spat out the first day we brought you here. She laughed and said, 'plant it, and may her reign be as fruitful.' And now it bears the most luscious olives."

Hypsipyle's heart lurched. The garden produced mixed emotions. Imbued with a sense of connection to her mother, it also accentuated her absence. Soon Hypsipyle's ache would include her father. She wanted to cry.

As they passed the old bee-wall, the hive buzzed with activity in the sun-warmed stones. Thoas paused. "Queen's gone," he informed her. "But the drones are still flying. The beekeeper said they'll keep working, even if they know they're doomed. Habit of survival, I suppose. You know, if you kill the drones before the queen lays again, there will be no next generation. Just sweetness left to rot in the comb."

Hypsipyle watched the bees. The irony of her father's observations did not escape her. She chastised her sensitivity. Not everything pertained to this evening's plan.

Arriving at a bend, they crossed a small footbridge arching over the stream. The sound of water tinkled, light and persistent. Thoas laughed to himself. He stopped and turned to Hypsipyle. "I argued this bridge needed to be stone." Hypsipyle met his grin. This too was another familiar story. "The old mason argued and said it would crack in flood if it couldn't sway. I didn't believe him, but we compromised. Used wood at the joints and look, it is still lasting. Longer than any of us expected. Fancy learning compromise from a mason."

Hypsipyle placed a hand on the rail. The water rushed below. She sought to lose herself in its swift movement, hoping to drown her despondency. She ached with a growing despair, every precious moment wasted by the burden of dominating thoughts.

Once over the bridge, a lolling hill challenged them. The physicality in struggling to the crest stole her capacity to think. Reaching the top, they sat panting to catch their breath. Noting a patch of scorched earth, Thoas pointed to where last season's weeds had been burned back. The charred scent lingered in the soil. "Lost half the oregano when we burned that." he explained. "Too easy to destroy more than you intend."

"What would you have done differently?" Hypsipyle asked.

"Maybe pull the weeds one by one. Slower. But more certain. You know what you're killing that way."

A hawk circled far above. They watched for a while then headed back down the hill. Nearing the courtyard, Thoas stopped beside a great stone altar, the flame still smouldering low from yesterday's rites.

"This flame isn't ours to keep, but to carry. The seer said, 'until she comes.' I asked of her identity, and he smiled at me. I think I understand now."

"Understand what, Patér?"

"That he didn't mean a warrior or a goddess. He meant someone who could rule with fire and restraint. Someone who could walk through the smoke, and still see clearly. He meant you, my dear. This kingdom is yours."

Hypsipyle stared into the flicker of flame. The silence between them amplified. Birds trilled in the distance, oblivious to the defining moment creeping upon her. Thoas moved closer, sensing something in her stillness. "What is it?"

Hypsipyle shook her head, unable to speak. Turmoil whirled inside her. She closed her eyes seeking calm, but the image of her father remained. How she loved him. How she trusted him. She looked up into his hooded brown eyes. "There is something I have to tell you."

She stared back into the coals. "The charred patch of earth. The bees. The bridge." Her words tumbled out lacking sense. How could she explain the garden turned oracle?

"We gathered. All of us. Not with rage, but with resolve. We have lived under coercion. Under bruises. Under their rules. So we decided, united as one. To reclaim Lemnos. To rid it of every man."

Thoas tugged at his beard. His confusion expressed in a grimace. "Even me?"

"Yes."

How to speak of something she did not understand? Some fragment or missing piece held the key to the circumstances holding Lemnos hostage. Iphinoe's suggestion of a curse carried a faint truth she was not privy to but could sense. "You are the crown. The root. If you remain," she paused at the euphemism. It did not protect her. "They will believe nothing has changed. That we chose mercy over justice."

Thoas understood this. "Mercy is the most dangerous weapon of all, Hypsipyle."

"I swore I would stand with them, that we stood in solidarity. I pledged to step beyond your shadow. We were united. Sisters. I promised I would not flinch."

Her hand curled into a fist, trembling. "But then you spoke of plucking weeds, and compromise, and the bees. As if you knew." She blinked, furious at the tears forming. "I don't know what choice to make. Either way, I betray someone I love."

Her admission hung between them. Long enough for shame to creep in. "They trust me to lead them. To destroy the old. To scorch the weeds."

Thoas took her fist and unfurled it flat in his hand. He laced their fingers. "You've changed your mind?"

"I saw you. Not as a king. Not as a man. As Patér. My Patér. The man who taught me to hold a blade. Who walked with me through every storm. The man who... who just ceded me his kingdom without knowing what I planned to do with it."

Thoas kissed her hand. "Don't lead them with vengeance. Lead with vision." He did not plead, but watched with a careful gaze to ascertain if her loyalty and love for him would prevail.

Hypsipyle stepped away. The garden swayed around her, its shades of green and gold indifferent to her turbulence. The rustle of the olive leaves, the steady hum of bees, and the water under the bridge conducted a symphony within her mind. The tremor in her words exposed her struggle. "If I save you," she said, "I betray my sisters. If I do nothing, I betray myself."

Her hand went to her throat. The air thickened. What would the women say? Their disbelief. Their fury. Their disappointment. She groaned loud and long, wanting to scream, wanting to expel all thought. She looked at Thoas. His stillness stoic and commanding, his trust unwavering.

"I believed we had to burn the whole field to kill the rot. But maybe we should cut carefully. Learn which roots still feed the soil." She stepped closer to confide to him, afraid of her words, afraid of her promise. "I won't let them kill you. I don't know what I'll tell them, or how I'll hide you, or if they'll ever forgive me. But I won't be the hand that ends you."

Thoas looked back at Hypsipyle. "Then you are already the Queen they need."

THOAS

Thoas left the garden, deep in thought. What the women were proposing was an abomination. 'How dare they rise up against us?' Treason to their country, their men, and to him, their King. He walked dazed and incredulous, sucked into a crucible of unfamiliar emotions. Distracted, he found himself at the doors of a small temple used to store the spoils of his accumulated victories.

Its entrance was framed by graceful archways. Solid marble pillars rose from a stepped stone base, their fluted shafts catching the sun's weary rays, throwing long shadows on the worn flagstones. Vines clung to the outer colonnade, their tendrils slipping through carved crevices. The scent of wild thyme graced the air.

A guard stood to attention. Thoas nodded and the man lifted the bar securing two large wooden doors, heaving them open before standing aside for his King to pass. Thoas glanced at the man with sudden understanding. He would be dead by dawn. An acknowledged fact. An objective, logical outcome on the basis of his daughter's confession. "Go home," Thoas ordered. The man startled, bowed low. Who was he to question the King? He left, not for home but the taverna.

Thoas stepped into the cool dim space. Inside, the polished floor, worn smooth by countless sandals, stood as a silent testament to earlier generations seeking quiet devotion, or perhaps wisdom and healing from a goddess whose modest statue he since moved to a far corner. He inhaled its aroma of reverence. Though small in scale, the temple exuded a quiet majesty appropriate to its transformation into his armory.

Thoas reigned in splendour, for Lemnos commanded the pathways of the northern Aegean trade, ensuring a steady flow of wealth and influence. He consolidated his authority with bronze of unmatched strength sourced from the fiery heat of Hephaestus' forge, guaranteeing success through military might.

Swords, knives, daggers, arrows; metal crafted by the God himself. Silver and bronze breastplates and helmets gleamed in memory of heroic deeds. Ah, what he had accomplished. He circled the room with his gaze taking stock. Trophies of war glittered around him. Bounties of gold and precious jewels stacked up against the left wall, complements of the cities he had raided, providing both honour and wealth. He sighed, seeing the sum worth of his life laid bare before him.

Leaving, he paused at the entrance, assessing the heavy doors. Did he care if his treasures were plundered? Only the men would be so bold, but their foolishness would be short lived. Their wives doling out their own punishment. He chuckled, then stopped short. He too would be dead if not for Hypsipyle.

An evening chill crept up from the sea as he strolled down the Avenue of Honour. While Dionysus shielded him with divine protection, his companions slain in battle were less fortunate and now represented by marble busts, carved with the love of true solidarity.

Memory took him further down the path. The wars he created, and those he defended, had been fought under the guise of honour, but Thoas knew the benefits of manufacturing warfare for reasons of economy and control. His wealth and power attested to this.

All combat was man-made. Men were responsible. And tonight

his men would die. Not with glory on the field, but in a domestic assault. Die an ignoble death in their beds. Killed by those they had protected and provided for. Hypsipyle spoke of betrayal, but who was betraying who? He knew the importance of respect and loyalty, these were virtues on the battlefield. What did a woman know of a man's love for himself or his brother? You measured a man's worth in combat. He stared at the line of statues, frozen in time, lost in a tribute no one would remember.

He had given his word he would not speak of the women's intentions. His silence in exchange for his life. He would forsake his brothers. Could he live with remorse?

War was an excellent teacher. Of course he could. He had killed without flinching; boys too young to hold a shield, civilians and innocent children. He had taken maidens before their first blood and mothers compliant to save their babes in arms. His courage and greatness among the bloodshed on the battlefield proved his honour, and his heroics well rewarded through plunder and pillage. He bore no regret in receiving accolades.

Tonight, there would be bloodshed, but it was not his war. He would comply, uphold his word and take his sleeping draught with full trust in his daughter. She possessed high principles, like her mother, and would never be unfaithful. If she intended to kill him, she would not have spoken of the plan.

He rubbed his arms to ward off the sharpness in the air and retraced his steps to the palace. He would awake from a peaceful sleep with an opportunity to begin life anew, to be rebirthed. He accepted his fate wholeheartedly.

THE MASSACRE

The women prepared a feast for their menfolk. The aroma of goat and pilaf baking in clay pots in the ovens of each home set mouths watering. The juices of male goat hid the bitter scent of sleep's eye flower. If it were known that this favourite dish was being served in every household, the men may have been forewarned something was amiss. But they took for granted the labours of their women and remained blinded by arrogance and a sense of entitlement. They exposed their folly by assuming there would be no repercussions for their behaviour toward either their wives or the Thracian women. Aphrodite had no need to meddle with this aspect embedded in the male psyche.

Hypsipyle visited her attendant Evthoxia to receive Thoas' portion. She watched Bendia, the Thracian woman who had replaced Evthoxia in her marriage bed, return the lid to the clay pot containing the meat. The small bowl of her father's ration sat ready on the table. As Hypsipyle entered, Bendia made her excuses and left the house.

"She knows?"

Evthoxia nodded. "Yes. She is overjoyed to be returning home. She has not seen her children for three years now."

"We are all complicit," Hypsipyle sighed. Her breach of trust tasted vitriolic. The decision she reached in the garden had not provided relief, on the contrary, it bullied her, tormenting and persecuting her with wretchedness. Taking her father's portion, she made ready to leave.

"The drays are ready to be loaded," Evthoxia advised. "I will see you tonight."

For a moment Hypsipyle became confused, then remembered. Of course, the catacombs. The two women hugged, offering silent support. Their shared touch acknowledged the multitude of conflicting feelings.

Her slow pace back to the palace enabled Hypsipyle to formalise a plan. Terrified of discovery, she grappled with the logistics of moving her father's body in secret. She did not fear death but the shame if caught. Every shadow whispered her story, deepening her anxiety, lest gossip reached those who could hear. Drugged into a sound sleep, Thoas' body might be too heavy for her to carry. Although strong, she could not leave this to chance. As she entered the gates she saw the cart bearing the statue of Dionysus. A solution presented itself.

"Patér?" She sought him out. "I have your dinner, and a plan."

Dressed for travel, Thoas sat in the cart and ate his food at the allocated time that the men would be eating. "You've grown into your mother's fire," he said. He stroked her cheek.

"No," she replied, "I've grown into something the world made."

Hypsipyle kissed his hand and covered him with blankets, straw and fresh flowers. By the time she harnessed the cart to one of the horses, muffled snoring could be heard. She then made her way to the Temple of Dionysus, travelling through the cobbled-stoned paths of the township crying for blessings from Dionysus to cleanse them of their violation.

Near the temple were several disused boats ready for Thoas to flee the island when he awoke.

*

The slaughter was silent. Knives sharpened by the men at the request of either their wives or concubines, sliced through flesh and bone. Some were decapitated as they slept. Others stabbed through the heart. For many, anger castrated a phallic trophy, chopped up into small pieces. Was murder supposed to be this easy?

The women of Lemnos retrieved prepared sacks from hiding places in the home and stuffed them with the bodies of the dead. The sound of dragging echoed through the village as women helped their neighbours lug the bags onto the drays. Conspiratorial murmurs entered houses while blood drenched matrimonial sheets, puddled on cool tiles or soaked into earthen floors.

The scent of jasmine hung in the air like a shroud, witness to the procession of women carting the bodies of their husbands, sons, brothers, fathers and uncles to the catacombs. Numbness crept alongside their slow march. The sight of the catacombs verified the reality of their nightmare, and mourning bewailed into the darkness of night. The deed was done.

Hypsipyle had arrived well ahead of the procession and her sack lay at the base of stone steps that descended into the catacomb. She left her cart off to one side, hoping to leave an impression she had received help with moving her father's body. Watching the drays being unloaded, with the sacks rolled off and smacking onto the ground, the lack of reverence annoyed her. Her father would have deserved more respect and for a moment she found satisfaction in her deceit.

The paved path into the giant cavern was worn thin to a pale pink by eons of shuffled feet. The curved archway delineated the light of the living from the shadows of the dead. Coolness permeated Hypsipyle's skin as the stone walls stood sentry, rigid against judgment. The path opened into a wide space, its walls carved with ledges and hollows, and filled with the bones of their ancestors. Death lingered, witnessing Hypsipyle's prayer to the gods to keep her deception safe.

Hypsipyle shook off offers of help and dragged her sack to her family's royal chamber. The smaller hollowed out section dug into the wall, offered privacy and enabled her to settle the sack deep in the recess. She scattered dirt and stones over it, thankful for this practice, for it hid the false shape of a bag stuffed with pebble-filled cushions.

"I wonder who will complete the mosaic?" The walls within the regal chamber were decorated with colourful images of her mother Myrina. Custom required this to be re-plastered and a new design incorporated when her father died, except the Royal Artisan now lay entombed in his own grave. Her idle thought shrivelled.

Leaving the catacombs, the women gathered at the entrance, hesitant to leave. Eyes darted, scanning the group for validation. They shared a pounding beat within their chests. As this quietened, a wave of euphoria washed through them. Astounded by the ease of their crime, a surge of victory splashed their disbelief. Realisation shone through the tumult. They had succeeded. The plan worked.

Previous class division between the women, once stark, now blurred with collaboration and the acknowledged atrocity of their act. The rich, swathed in aromas of privilege and power, and the poverty stricken, bedraggled and putrid, who slept in gutters with companions of death, corruption and brutality, united. Status became irrelevant. No longer superior or worthless or subject to adoration or vendetta, the divide between them diminished by deed. Guilt became their common denominator.

THE ERINYES

A hideous cackle rose from the bowels of the earth as the three sisters, Tisiphone, Megaera and Alecto, retreated to the hollows of the Erebus, smacking their lips in glee. Snakes hissed and spat as phantoms whirled in the draft created from their exuberant entrance into gloom. Their exclamations and raucous recounting of their deed overlapped in cacophonous screeching, howling and guttural expletives.

"Did you see it sisters?"

"That we did."

"Where shadows cling to root and bone, where the ground remembers every drop of blood ever spilled." With odious breath the Erinyes sniggered with hateful satisfaction.

"She wanted vengeful destruction. She got it."

"A poisonous hum in the marrow of silence stirred sleeping embers."

"Into the smoke that rose from their hearths, kissing their furrowed brows. Ripening their rage."

"Oh pity, pity, their little forlorn hearts, blistered from treachery."

"They had not broken oaths. The oaths were broken to them."

"And so, we came. And justice meted out."

"Yes, yes."

"We came to witness. Those scorned and buried beneath the weight of a man's name."

"They burned the weeds."

"Cleared the rot from their garden, they did." They shrieked with malicious delight at their joke and it took some time for the sisters to settle. Their ecstasy and hilarity fuelled their tirade as they sucked delight from the nightmare that had befallen Lemnos.

"And now they carry ash upon their skin like war paint."

"We did that. We marked them."

"And it will not stop."

"The reckoning does not end with the blade. It begins in the blood that is spared."

Throughout the night the sisters continued to retell their tale, consumed by the evil pleasure wreaked from their curse.

THE MORNING AFTER

Helios smelt the odour of death, and reluctant to discover its source, dawdled into the day. The hush of Lemnos weighed heavy in dazed silence. The streets were empty. The wind snaked its way through alleyways, afraid to linger.

Hypsipyle waited alone in the town square. Sleep eluded her. She heard the silence from Dionysus' temple louder than any scream. Mercy, she feared, might yet be the seed of her undoing.

She wore her father's regal purple cloak, woven by the Graces for Dionysus who presented it to Thoas, after Rhadamanthus bequeathed him Lemnos. Hers now. Heir to the throne. Queen of Lemnos.

Iphinoe arrived first, saving Hypsipyle from slipping into any abusive self-judgement. "It is done," Iphinoe sighed. "Last night," she leaned close, her voice low, "did you hear the laughter of the Erinyes?" Hypsipyle baulked. She looked at Iphinoe aggrieved and shook her head. Alkippe's approach prevented further conversation. Her face streaked with ash and her red eyes told a tale of sleepless grief. More women joined. No one spoke. No one laughed. No one wept. Not anymore. A new day had begun.

Hypsipyle watched the crowd swell. Killers. Survivors. Sisters. She walked to the top of the temple steps with Pollyx beside her. She gazed upon the upturned faces. Drained, tired, others had not slept either. Many women clasped hands. Some wore widow weeds.

"Together we rebuild our lives." she said to them. "Their

bodies lie in the catacomb, not as heroes but as men we once loved. And when we build again," Hypsipyle continued, her voice steady though her throat ached. "it will be not of the past, but something new."

The island had turned. The women, weary, wild, and free, stood together, not redeemed, but rebirthed.

APHRODITE

The air shimmered in Aphrodite's garden from her beauty so intense roses bloomed and withered in the same breath. The goddess reclined beneath a myrtle tree older than time. Its smooth bark gleamed like polished pearl. Pale blossoms opened with the hush of secrets best left unspoken. Its glossy leaves dappled the surface of a shallow pool next to her. She traced a finger through the water watching her own reflection ripple and reform. Perfection.

A slight draft of wings heralded a messenger. Feathered. Fast. He descended. She was disappointed it was not Hermes, for they could have enjoyed some banter. Some minor wind spirit alighted, a youthful winged one whose name she may have known but easily forgot. This young thing trembled in the glow of her gaze. He knelt, head low "My lady," he sighed, "it is done."

Aphrodite rolled her eyes. "Speak."

"The women of Lemnos have acted. They drugged their husbands and slew them as they slept. All but one. Thoas, father of Hypsipyle, lives, hidden by his daughter."

"I see," said Aphrodite. Her voice discordant, yet honey smooth.

The messenger dared a glance. "Your curse has played out."

She laughed. "A curse? Is that what they call it?"

He lowered his head. "It is what the Erinyes called it. Your request has been answered."

Aphrodite rose. The garden shifted with her as flowers craned to her touch. "I asked for reckoning," she said. "For the scales to tremble with justice. For love, slighted and spat upon, to be remembered in flesh, not just fading sighs." She walked past him, the rustle of her silk robes serenading her movement.

"I am not to blame," she said. "Look to Hephaestus, God of bonds. Maker of chains for hearts and hands alike. It was he who forged the marriage bed cold as iron. He who left desire to rot in the mouths of mortal men."

She turned. Her eyes blazed. "Do you know what that does to me? When the sacred spark I gift is mocked, ignored, twisted into duty?"

"No, my lady." The winged messenger had no escape. He bowed lower so as not to catch her wrath.

"Of course you do not." She snapped. She smoothed her robes. "You said one did not kill?"

"Hypsipyle spared her father."

"Mercy, or cowardice?"

"The message bears no judgment."

"No," said Aphrodite, her eyes narrowing. "Pity. Even the most beautiful stories stumble at mercy."

Aphrodite turned back to the pool. The surface glimmered as a vision rose. She looked upon Lemnos, washed in pale morning light. Women standing together. One figure stood out. 'That must be Hypsipyle, with her hands so clean but her soul marked,' she guessed.

"Let them call it wrath," said Aphrodite, turning to the messenger. "Let them weep and sing dirges and bind their hair in grief. But what they did was love. Not the soft kind. The kind with teeth. Now leave."

Aphrodite stirred the water. "How does it feel, husband of mine, to carry the blame for this deed. This blood is on your hands. These women will mock you at your own Temple." She felt a sense of accomplishment, and yet it was still so early in the day.

JASON

At first it appeared as a blemish on the horizon. A smudge moving too straight to be mistaken for an albatross and too swift to be driftwood. It drew closer, cleaving the sea with deliberate grace. Long and low, it sliced through the water. The women, used to galleys of various sizes, were awed by the approaching vessel. It was a monster of the sea.

Its large, central sail, raised high on the mast, billowed in a favourable wind. The sun's rays cast a creamy, golden hue through it. Rows of long oars moved its oaken hull in rhythm as if timed to a beat. A red pennant flew from the masthead as it glided across the surface. Toward Lemnos. Coming within sight, men could be seen clustered under a canopy toward the stern.

Hypsipyle urged the women to don the armour of their men, ready to fight to maintain their freedom. They stood on the dock sheathed in bronze breastplates and helmets. All except those too old, too frail or too young were prepared for battle in armour that didn't fit and hung too broad at the shoulders. Worse, it bore the stench of their men, weighted with memory. Helmets obscured their faces. Eyes gleaned through slits like wary animals.

Hypsipyle stood at the front of the women. Her helmet, too big and heavy, lopped side to side with any movement. It demanded effort not to tilt her head. Her breastplate constricted her movements. How did men ever fight in these contraptions? "We do not know who they are. But we know what men bring. Fire. Blades. Arrogance. Let them find no softness here."

Pollyx approached. She wore no armour. "Hypsipyle," she called, making her way through the gathering.

"The tide has brought strangers. We defend what we've made." The women cheered as Hypsipyle raised her sword.

"Hypsipyle, if I may counsel?"

"Of course."

Pollyx spoke with a breathless urgency. "You saw the boat. It does not bear the hallmarks of war. No shields line the rails, no telltale glint of bronze. No cattle carts. It moves steadily, but not with the urgency of conquest, more the weariness of distance. I think it is a trader's vessel or perhaps seafarers seeking harbour."

"All men come with hunger in their mouths."

"And what if they come with hope? What if this is not a second ending, but a chance to begin again. This time on our terms?"

"With respect, Pollyx, we began again after we filled the catacombs. We are already living the second beginning."

"Are we? Or are we trapped in ash." Pollyx stepped closer and lowered her voice. "We dress in their armour, Hypsipyle. Not to protect ourselves, but because we still bear their burden. We carry their weight. Their rules. Their war."

As Hypsipyle considered her words, Pollyx continued. "Let us meet these strangers not with fear disguised as rage, but with the power we have forged. Let us decide the story, not by striking first, but by choosing how to receive them."

Hypsipyle hesitated. Pollyx reasoned well.

"If they mean harm..." Hypsipyle began.

Pollyx cut her off. "Then we show them the strength of women who have survived before. But don't you see? If we meet war with war, we mirror the world we left behind. We become like them. Let these men prove themselves, or condemn themselves. But let it be their choice, not our presumption."

Hypsipyle removed her helmet and dropped it to the ground. The elder spoke wise words. She turned to the assembly before her. "We will not fight. Let them come. We are not afraid of peace." The muted thud of metal on earth resounded the women's relief.

In silence they watched. Tense. They had killed their men and buried their past. And now men returned, rowed by the tide. Who were these men? Warriors? Traders? Invaders? What gods sent them? And what would they demand in return? No one spoke, but questions hung thick.

Hypsipyle stood at the fore with Pollyx, Alkippe and Iphinoe by her side. As a smaller row boat approached, Hypsipyle addressed the band of men it carried. "You sail under no known banner. Your ship is armed, your crew all men. State your purpose or be cast into the sea."

The leader, a young handsome man, looked up at Hypsipyle. His tunic clung damp to his muscular chest. "I am Jason, son of Aeson, rightful heir to the throne of Iolcus. We are not raiders, Queen, nor foes to Lemnos. It is passage and provision we seek."

Hypsipyle felt an unfamiliar stirring in her loins. Its intensity played a distracting game. She glared at him, this stranger who provoked such a response. Her cold reply sought to contain her reaction. "Provisions for what? A war? A hunt? We've seen men hunt what they do not understand."

"Not a war. A quest. We sail to Colchis, across the dark throat of the Euxine Sea. There lies the Golden Fleece, the skin of a sacred ram, guarded by sleepless dragons. I go to claim it, not for greed, but to reclaim my birthright as King."

Hypsipyle frowned. "You would risk your life for a pelt?"

"Not for the fleece. For justice." He stood before her, young, bold, golden. A mortal god. She clenched her legs, alarmed by the effect he had on her. His yellow locks flickered with specks of gold, catching the sun and stealing her breath. She had never known a man to be so beautiful. She fought to remain calm and composed while inside everything pulsed and throbbed and swirled. She fought a desire to rub her body against his. Was this love? She became aware of everyone's focus on her, waiting for her response. She studied him to find fault. Words from her father came to her aid. "Danger has many faces. You say you are no threat, yet storms follow the heels of men with something to prove."

"We come with oars, not swords. If you have suffered at the hands of men, let us be different. Judge us by our deeds. When we depart we will leave only footprints on the sand."

"Words are easier to spill than blood."

"Then watch me bleed, Queen. But know this, I did not cross Poseidon's fury to deceive the people of Lemnos."

"Then let the gods test your truth," she replied. "This is the sacred land of Hephaestus and chamber of Aphrodite. You may come ashore. But if you mean harm, Lemnos will not weep when the tide takes you back."

Jason stared dumbstruck. Hypsipyle, with her braided hair tied back, in bulky armour that emphasised a youthful vulnerability, was delectable. He licked the salt from his lips at the mention of Aphrodite, goddess reigning over love and passion and pleasure. He would pay tribute tenfold. "If the tide takes me, it won't be because I failed to honour your trust," he answered.

In a hushed tone, Iphinoe reminded Hypsipyle of her obligations. "Whoever comes to your home as a guest, treat them as a god, for so they may be."

"Yes," Hypsipyle agreed, and turning back to Jason, welcomed him. "May your enemy never host you, nor you your enemy. You may camp on the beach. I will provide a banquet to receive you and your men."

*

The Argo nudged the shore, scraping timber on sand. The ramp lowered into the shallows and the men disembarked. Jason watched as Hypsipyle left the dock. His eyes swept across the crowd as they turned and followed their Queen. He realised all were women. Hercules followed his gaze. The great lion pelt shifted on his shoulders. "Where are the men?"

Jason shrugged, entranced by Hypsipyle, still in view. "They must be further inland. Working the fields, perhaps."

Hercules glanced around. "Not a single pair of sandals in the sand but ours." He squinted at two figures walking separate from the main group. One, still in a bronze breastplate and a helmet tucked under her arm, and the other dressed in a simple tunic but holding herself with command. They both turned and looked toward the boat before continuing their journey. "Do you feel it?"

Jason nodded. "Something is wrong."

"I'd wager a year's wine and two of Orpheus's songs that it's something to do with what's missing." Hercules frowned. "There are no men. Or youths"

The atmosphere turned ominous. Jason trusted Hercules' warrior instincts, and agreed. "We stay cautious. Be gracious guests. Until we know more."

THE PLAN

The walls of Aphrodite's Temple glowed with firelight. Offerings of figs, honey, and burnt sage smouldered on low braziers. A statue of the Goddess looked on from the far end. Carved in pale marble, her face serene with observant eyes.

Hypsipyle stood before her. The sway of lust within had awakened something dormant and her emotions were an entangled mesh of confusion. She prayed to the Goddess for help.

Iphinoe sat at a low altar lighting candles of bees wax. They had agreed to meet with Pollyx before joining their guests on the beach. Music floated up, and often the loud laughter of men erupted into the evening, somewhat jarring. As Pollyx entered the Temple, Iphinoe rose to greet her. The three women sat together on stone seats inlaid into the walls.

"You wish to talk? About the men?" Hypsipyle trusted their counsel.

"It is. And it isn't," replied Iphinoe.

"You've seen them," Pollyx said. "Healthy. Strong. Not one a boy or elder. They're a gift. If we choose to see it."

"A gift? Or a threat wrapped in bronze?" Hypsipyle did not trust her instincts given her unprecedented yearning.

Iphinoe explained. "That depends on how we receive them. Aphrodite's Temple has gone too long without celebration. Without purpose. The Goddess grows restless. She speaks to me in my dreams."

The distant hum from the beach wafted into the space. Pollyx tilted her head to listen. "They expect hospitality. Let us give them spectacle. We hold a contest, games where they can compete in feats of strength, wit, and charm. In Aphrodite's honour."

"And we reward the victors," Iphinoe added. "With our bodies."

"With our choice." Pollyx clarified. "We are not cattle. We choose the winners. We set the rules. And yes, we give them what they desire, while we take what we need."

"What do we need, pray tell, Pollyx?" asked Hypsipyle.

"Impregnation," Pollyx answered. "To restore balance. To fill our cradles so Lemnos can flourish."

"So we dress it in devotion and call it holy?"

"Is there a difference? We need a future. And that means children. Sons and daughters. Sired by warriors, raised by us."

Hypsipyle looked back at Aphrodite's statue. The flickering light animated her carved smile. Had the Goddess answered her prayer?

"Games, it will be." said Hypsipyle. "Let the gods witness and the women decide.

MELITTA

A crescent moon hung in a velvet sky. It provided little light for the women walking to Aphrodite's Temple. Being the first major community gathering since that fateful night, many were agitated by memories and apprehensive as they stepped into the torch-lit space. A subdued hum stretched out from the Argonauts' beach camp. At this late hour, the warriors were settling in for the night.

Iphinoe welcomed them, reminding them to keep their voices low. Pollyx and Alkippe stood at the altar as the pale marble statue of Aphrodite watched on. Flowers were strewn around her base and libations of wine and honey were offered to all.

Hypsipyle stood aside in quiet conversation with Melitta, a mature woman who she knew to be thoughtful, wise and kind. As Hypsipyle took her place next to the elders, Melitta slipped outside and sat on the stone steps. The large wooden doors of the temple remained ajar as the murmur of discussion wove its way outside.

A rustle of a shrub, the slide of gravel underfoot alerted her to a presence. Melitta stood. Hypsipyle had guessed correctly. "Enter the light," she demanded.

A tall man dressed in a simple tunic presented himself. "I bring no threat," he reassured, opening his arms to show he carried no weapon. "I am Hylas, servant of Hercules."

"Why are you here? Trespassing on sacred ground in the dark. It is beyond your camp and where you have not been invited."

"I saw the torchlight," he answered. "Curiosity drew me here to learn whether this temple honours Hephaestus or Aphrodite. My intention is to pay homage to Hephaestus, to pray for courage to hold my sword steady on the battlefield when we reach Colchis. I prefer to hide my fear from my colleagues in the shadow of darkness."

"Hylas, you say?" Melitta studied him. A little thin, a little young, but a warrior, nonetheless. "Do you consider yourself a stallion, or somewhat more tender? Your name is smooth on the tongue." A twinkle of mirth shone from her eyes causing him to pause. In the moonlight, Melitta seemed transformed into the Goddess herself. Her robes draped in a silken flow over her ample breasts. Hylas quivered. The Goddess of Love called to him but he was unsure how to respond.

Melitta watched him carefully. She saw his hesitation, his slight confusion and his desire. She reached out her hand. "My name is Melitta. In the absence of our men, I have been unable to fulfil my duties to Aphrodite. I fear I have neglected her. Would you be willing to assist me in paying homage to the Goddess of Love, Beauty, Pleasure, Passion, and Procreation?"

Hylas stared at her outreached hand and swallowed. His words tumbled out as he accepted her invitation. "Yes. Of course. I am no stallion, Melitta, but an Argonaut. A man of honour and valour. It is my pleasure to pay homage and participate in the worship of Aphrodite with you."

Melitta led him away from the Temple to a small clearing with cushioned grass underfoot. He sunk to the ground with Melitta in his arms.

Their passion spent, they watched the stars shimmer against an infinite black backdrop. Melitta got up and attended her robes. Hylas propped himself on his elbow, watching her with tenderness. "Where are your men?" he asked with a feigned casual interest.

Melitta bit back a smile. Hypsipyle had prepared her for this. She offered her hand to help Hylas to his feet. He rose and embraced her. She led him down a trail toward the beach taking an equally casual approach to answer him. "Our men sailed off on a raid, on a quest that failed. Many were killed or enslaved, and those that returned brought back a disease unknown to our island. We quarantined them, but over time they preferred to take their chances and chose freedom on the open seas. They elected to forsake Hephaestus and conceded their oath to Poseidon. We watched them sail away. They will never return."

Hylas nodded. "Has it been difficult? To live without men?"

"At first, yes. We grieved them. But today we fish and farm and provide for ourselves. We are strong and healthy. We too love our freedom."

They kissed farewell with fondness amid a chorus of grunts and snores and the flicker of dying coals from campfires scattered along the shore. Melitta returned to the Palace to share her story with Hypsipyle. It had been a fortuitous evening, and she glowed with satisfaction.

JASON'S DEPARTURE

Lying with legs entangled on the plush day bed, Hercules poked Jason with his foot. "It is time to go. The women are sated and will soon produce heirs to their lands. We have dallied too long. Let us proceed with our quest."

Jason eyed the toned taut body of his lover and nodded. Bedding the Queen had been an unexpected bonus, but a distraction, nevertheless. His destiny belonged in Thessaly as the rightful King of Iolcus. His uncle's taunt echoed in his ears: "To take my throne, which you shall, you must go on a quest to find the Golden Fleece." Jason sat up and scratched his groin. "Assemble the crew, we leave at tomorrow's dawn." Slipping into his tunic, he went to find Hypsipyle. Time to turn on the charm.

He came upon her tending the garden and gathering herbs. He watched her with impassionate disdain. She had been an easy conquest. "Here," he offered, taking her basket. She stretched her back. The weight of her protruding belly was onerous. In less than two full moons she would be delivered from her body's burden. It seemed like an eternity.

Jason set down the basket and wrapped her in his arms. He felt her quiver with his touch. He ran his fingers down her spine, eliciting a moan. His broad smile disguised his smirk as he nuzzled into the vulnerability of her exposed neck. "My love," she murmured, pleasured by his embrace.

"My love," Jason echoed. He raised her chin and brushed her lips with his. He had mastered the art of seduction. "Hercules has received word, and the winds are in our favour. We will board the Argo at dawn and continue our quest. The Fleece must be retrieved."

Hypsipyle sucked in air with an abrupt force. She had anticipated this moment, but why so soon? "Beloved, my time is nigh. Do you not wish to be presented with the fruit of your loin? The child you desire?" Her mind scrambled in search of a strategy. Why choose to leave now? It was too soon. She was unprepared. Her heart fractured, its brittle pieces falling on to the grassy path. Her knees buckled.

Jason held her. She rested her head upon his chest and listened to the strong beat within, its rhythm attuned to the exploits of men.

"It is not forever," he promised. "You bestow my life with purpose and glory. Not the sea nor the will of kings will keep me from coming back to you."

"You promised to stay and protect us. Yet you choose another promise to prioritise." Did she believe him? Did she have a choice? "You can be King here," she suggested. She would not plead, but she could hope.

"I have my destiny. I will reclaim my kingdom. I am no Queen's lapdog," Jason replied. Hypsipyle drew on her remaining strength to stand aside and take Jason's hands. She placed them on her belly. "If not for me..."

"No, my love. As you are no doubt aware, if the child is male, it my heir. When it is born, my attendant Eurimedes will take it to my mother to be raised in Iolcus. If a girl, it is yours."

"A girl is more worthy," she snapped. "Do you not remember the midwife says I bear two?"

"Then two sons will be returned." His words softened. "I will come back to you. I promise."

Hypsipyle could see he would not be swayed. She straightened her shoulders and regaining her poise answered, "I will make preparations for your departure." She turned to spare him from her tears.

*

The moon cast silver streaks across the courtyard as torches blazed, sending dancing shadows over tables groaning under the weight of platters piled high with roasted lamb, honey-glazed figs, olives and breads. The sweet melody of a lyre tugged at Hypsipyle's emotions. Despite her gaiety and bursts of laughter, she wore a cloak of heaviness.

Sitting at the head of a long table, her gaze drifted to Jason beside her. Committing him to memory, she drank in his golden hair and sun-kissed skin, his handsomeness and heroic bearing. The scent of the seas, of salt and pine, clung to him despite his time on the island. Aware of her scrutiny, he smiled, tender and brief. He was already looking toward the horizon.

"My Queen," called Orpheus from further down the table, "you honour us beyond measure. In every harbour hence, your name shall sail with us."

"Then let the wine flow as freely as your songs, Orpheus," Hypsipyle replied. "Let this night be one of joy, not of counting losses."

The women of Lemnos raised their cups to the Argonauts, who were boisterous with celebration. They were men of the sea, too long had they remained on land. Hercules sat apart. He had been unable to discover the truth about the island's inhabitants. The explanation Hylas present seemed too expedient. It had not bothered Jason, but an island devoid of men struck him as an anomaly. The stars had kept their silence.

When the torches burned low, Hypsipyle stood to address the gathering. All chatter ceased as faces turned to her. "I would speak," she said. "Not as Queen, but as woman. You came to us when our home was silent and grieving. You brought laughter and desire, as well as the chaos of men." Amused chuckles from the table masked the falter in her voice. "We furnished you with shelter, our beds, and our trust. Tomorrow, you return to your quest. Such is the way of heroes. We wish you godspeed."

Jason reached for her hand, "I will not forget you."

"I hope not," she said. She leaned toward him, "but I do not wait."

The music resumed, low and wistful, fading the night's reveries. As Hypsipyle headed toward her chamber, Jason joined her. Together in step, their thoughts took different journeys. Hypsipyle broke the silence. "Will your travels take you near an island called Anthemoessa?"

"We head toward the land of the Dolines, and then make our way to Colchis. The Golden Fleece is hanging on a sacred tree in the grove of Ares. The island you speak of is not in the vicinity. Why do you ask?"

"I heard of some sisters transformed into half bird women by the Goddess Demeter. Companions of Persephone, they were with her when she entered the Underworld. Demeter gave them wings to search for her. When they returned with knowledge of Persephone's fate, Demeter blamed them for not looking after her and punished them."

Hypsipyle stopped to look upon her beloved. "Keeping their half-bird wings and legs, Demeter set them upon a small rocky outcrop and cursed them with immortality to forever call for Persephone. Their lamentation is entrancing because their voices appeal to the spirit, not the flesh. It is so lovely, no one can resist." Looking at Jason, she knew he would not resist any enticement of a beautiful woman. Spirit or flesh.

"Sailors lured by the Sirens song all die. They crash their ships onto the rocks. Or if they navigate onto the shore of the rocky island, the Sirens song laps both body and soul in a fatal lethargy, and the men starve to death."

Jason took her hand and they continued walking.

"But if someone hears their singing and lives, the Sirens will be released from Demeter's curse." As soon as Hypsipyle spoke, she regretted her words. Of course Jason would take up the challenge. That's what heroes did.

"I have heard of these seducers of men," Jason replied. "But I heard they were proud and challenged the Muses to a singing contest. The Muses won and plucked their feathers to use as crowns. Being featherless and white in their nakedness, the Sirens threw themselves into the sea. A nearby town claimed the name Aptera for them, and small islets in the bay are called the Leukai. But this is on Kriti, where the bronze giant Talos lives. We will not be travelling so far south."

"Then I have no need for concern," Hypsipyle said. She looked up to the charcoal heavens. Stars glistened like teardrops. "Have you everything you require? Can I ease your departure?"

"There is nothing more to do my love but share this night in revelry." He kissed her hand, and despite the weight within her womb, she too longed for his promise of pleasure.

*

Dawn kissed open the empty silence of night. Helios appeared too eager as he commenced his daily sojourn, surprising the roosters with his haste. The dock transformed into an emotional cauldron mixing trepidation and excitement with sorrow and relief. As Hypsipyle handed Jason her sacred purple robe as a parting gift, she spoke cautionary words, "If our parting is the end of our journey together, and your shadow rests not upon this land forevermore, be warned. If you seek to exploit my passion to serve your own interests, you will suffer the fate of the Panderer and Seducer. In the upper half of the Hell of the Fraudulent and Malicious, you shall be whipped by horned daemons for all of eternity."

Jason shook off her curse with an endearing smile, conjuring false tears of loss and regret. He took her hand and raised it to his lips. "My Queen Hypsipyle, love of my being, mother to my children, we will share the many tomorrows of our future and side by side we shall grow old and reap the harvest of our love. We will be nourished by the pleasures and memories of these twilight hours together. But for now, Sirus beckons. I leave you my heart for safe keeping. I will return to reclaim it once I fulfill my mission and the stars align."

While royal etiquette demanded a formal departure, the crowd around them erupted with wild abandon. Men and women lunged at one another, kissing and grappling, entwined in urgent farewell. Some women, not yet swollen with seed, leapt onto eager lovers, their cries charged with ecstasy. Laughter and moans orchestrated a chorus of release. Hair tumbled loose, robes slid from shoulders, garlands snapped beneath trampling feet. The air thickened with sweat, salt, and the heady scent of lust. The dock dissolved into a frenzy of passion and parting.

As the Argo sailed from sight, the women heaved a collective sigh of relief. Sex may be great, but they rejoiced in their freedom to live unhindered by the demands of men.

HYPSIPYLE'S TORMENT

With idle time since both Jason and her babies left Lemnos many moons of heartbreak ago, a conspiracy of shame, remorse and grief worked in stealth to transform Hypsipyle. Once a brilliant blue sky, radiant with the carefree gold of the sun, she descended into a brooding, ominous day. At first, vapour wisps drifted in, their thin silver-grey haunting too weak to cast shadows. But ignoring their flimsy warning fed the beast. Clouds grew heavy, crowding the edges of her conscience. Low, dark, and thunderous, the sky pressed in too close, suffocating her with accusations. Guilt conquered each waking day. She withdrew into herself.

Days were tolerable when spent alone, as self-recrimination became the mainstay of her inner monologue. Every face that looked upon her, glowing with honesty, faith and integrity, fed her disgrace and self-disgust. 'I should have stood with them, bloodied and sure.' Her smile was as falsified as her honour. 'They look at me with trust in their eyes. Sister, they say. And I lie. Not with words, but silence. With my hands empty when theirs are red.'

It took little effort to mask her shame with the sorrow of the loss of her babies. She had nursed them for one full moon until wrenched away. Two swarthy twin boys, like little Jasons, who made her heart both sing and scream in a silent twisting of a knife through her soul. But she did not fool herself. She felt a wave of relief watching their boat disappear into the blur between sky and horizon. Her children would have been raised on the milk of a traitor, in a home of deception, where truth slunk into corners holding her hostage with the threat of divulging her insidious secret. They deserved better. Now she could close off her heart.

Speaking with caution, Pollyx intruded into Hypsipyle's seclusion. "My Queen, I am concerned. You have withered and grown morose since the babies left. May I intercede on your behalf and have Aethra call upon you?"

It registered that her old nurse distanced herself and spoke with formality. Hypsipyle ignored the lifeline, wishing it were an anchor to drown her instead. "I am fine, Pollyx. Thank you. I think I'll get some fresh air." She stood and reached for her shawl.

Pollyx watched from the doorway, her face furrowed with disquiet. "When did we lose you?" Her muttered words were lost within the heavy shroud of gloom surrounding her former charge.

Hypsipyle walked to the Temple of Dionysus. Her afternoon pilgrimage enabled her to hide while in the village, the women flourished with the prosperity of freedom. They worked hard learning new skills on both sea and land. Life may have been tough, but they rejoiced in their liberty and accomplishments. In a purgatory of her own design, Hypsipyle did not have the capacity to appreciate the sunny disposition of this burgeoning community. Disloyalty had no place.

She sat on the temple steps, numb to the stone's coldness. She stared at the disused boats, one missing with only its imprint on the sand left to fling bold accusations of treachery. No-one had noticed. She wondered, as she did each day, did Thoas live? The memory of him wrapped in blankets, hidden in the cart like a secret no oath could sanctify, provided no answer. She stared out to sea. It shimmered, showing off its beauty. Inviting her in. 'If only,' she wished, 'I could be cleansed that easily.'

She could not prevent a cascade of clamouring thoughts.

'What was I thinking? That the gods would turn away? That the scent of blood would mask my silence? I may not have lifted a blade, but I killed truth. Tucked it away beneath straw and linen. As if I was different. That sparing him was an act of grace. Mercy is the worst betrayal.' The women had trusted her and looked her in the eye with blood on their hands and called her sister.

The sparkle of the sea beckoned and for a moment she wanted nothing more than to offer herself to Poseidon. But even he could not purify her stench of falsehood. Life become a prison, cloaked by deed, disloyalty and dishonour. She was an unworthy Queen. No crown could redeem what she had done. 'It is I that should be on my knees begging forgiveness.'

A small bird fluttered in front of her, pecking at the dirt, hunting for seed. She watched with envy. Oh, to be a bird. "Begone bird, take your happiness elsewhere." The bird flew off at the sound of her voice.

Her breast dribbled milk despite the herbs from Aethra. She rubbed her chest then hunched over, hugging her knees, and squinted into the sea haze. "What to do?" she asked no-one. The voice in her head responded. 'Do something.' She sighed in agreement.

She watched a trail of ants as they trudged up the stone carrying the body of a dead comrade. Working together, they shared the weight, shouldering burdens born of loyalty. She saw herself as that dead ant. But undeserving of being carried. Hers was a burden of betrayal. Alienated from their solidarity, she set herself apart when she decided to save Thoas. She chose wrong. A reckoning dawned. She needed to face the consequence of her choice. Take accountability. Learn to carry herself once more.

"Yes," she exclaimed standing with new purpose. 'Their rage will be righteous.' She pulled her shawl over her shoulders. Hers was not a matter for Poseidon. Let the women decide her fate.

55

JUDGEMENT

Hypsipyle summoned the community to the partially constructed amphitheatre, where the work, while not complete, provided a suitable stage for a grand drama. The audience would not be disappointed.

As Pollyx assisted Hypsipyle in getting ready, she sensed something momentous stirring. Arriving at the site, she squeezed Hypsipyle's hand. "Take care dear Queen, for as you know words are like seeds on the breeze. Once released, they drift beyond your reach and take root where they will." She took her seat next to Alkippe and other elders. All women were in attendance.

Hypsipyle trembled, overcome with the enormity of her intention. It had been an arduous journey to reach this decision, demanding her to explore every shadow she harboured with the purpose of aligning her values. Values that laid buried under her dishonesty, lies and duplicity. Standing in front of the women, fear consumed her. She was worse than worthless, the lowest form of scum. How dare she hold a place of love from these women?

Despite the warmth of the day, cold sweat glistened on her brow. The knot in her stomach reached into her throat, clogging her breath. Contaminated blood pulsed through her veins. An apology could never measure the weight of her regret, for her remorse dwelled in an abyss untouched by gods or mortals.

She could not look up. Not yet. She tried to raise her head, but the intensity of her repugnance dragged it down again. She turned away, then back again. The dirt ground of the amphitheatre had flecks of limestone scattered in its mix.

Hypsipyle focused on them. She breathed in a rhythm of long and deep breaths to help find composure. 'At least let me be honest with myself. I can do that.' The earth felt solid, it offered solace. Time was patient.

She closed her eyes and scanned her body. Her feet felt supported and grounded. She breathed into her sacral region, acknowledging the strength required to face retribution. She felt her solar plexus flare. Its brilliant yellow glow feeding her with confidence and purpose. She raised her hands to her chest. 'Always lead with love,' she reminded herself. She addressed her choked throat, reaffirming, 'I will speak my truth with clarity and fearless grace.'

Women coughed their discomfort. Waiting. Emotions swirled in a vortex. No-one possessed the strength to make eye connect. Bravery has dissipated. Distance offered a safety zone, and while some women shifted in their seats, others wrapped their arms around themselves and rocked. Whatever Hypsipyle planned, everyone knew it would not be good.

Raising her head, Hypsipyle reassured herself, 'I trust my vision.' She looked up to the big blueness of sky. Majestic and beautiful, she soaked in its loveliness and affirmed, 'courage flows through me from a source greater than fear.'

Walking into the centre of the amphitheatre, she positioned herself midway between the poles of isolation and engulfment. There, Hypsipyle made eye contact with every woman in the arena waiting for her to speak. She swallowed back the sensation of tears welling behind her eyes. She would be ruthless and would earn back her self-respect.

She began. "Shame has grown in the shadow of my silence. As has guilt, fear, distress and contempt. I speak my disgrace in full knowledge I carve a distance that will separate us forever.

It cannot be undone. I refuse the mantle of victim. I admit to being afraid. Afraid to speak, afraid to be judged, but there is no other recourse and so ..." Hypsipyle knelt in the dirt, "I beg your forgiveness. I do not trust mercy and do not plead for it. I believe in justice. Sisters behold this woman, not fit to be your Queen lest I lead you into unmarked paths paved with corruption. I beg you bear witness that I no longer avoid taking responsibility. No longer will I mask my shame. Nor deceive you."

She stood. "King Thoas did not die alongside your menfolk. I spared his life and facilitated his escape."

The amphitheatre became a tomb of stillness. Shock descended, encasing them all. As comprehension settled in its wake, reaction awoke. Women gasped. Many covered their faces. Others frowned with intense concentration, while some held their ears, not wishing to hear such woe from their beloved Queen. But no attempt to mute her words could diminish her honest truth. She betrayed them.

Alkippe stood. All eyes turned to her. Her restrained request voiced a simple direction. "Return to your chamber Hypsipyle. We will call for you once we have discussed this."

*

Pollyx did not attend Hypsipyle. Stepping out into a pastel dusk that cast a veil over the land, Hypsipyle followed an unknown maiden back to the amphitheatre to learn of her fate. A hushed sorrow greeted her as she entered the arena. Alkippe, Iphinoe and Pollyx stood waiting. Hypsipyle approached them, her head bowed.

Alkippe spoke. "We acknowledge and witness your humility and guilt. While you may not have taken up a blade, we accept you shared our distress and grief of that murderous night. We also acknowledge that you led us from our crime and introduced a new way to live. You guided our journey through rebirth so we grew strong and resourceful, that we now reap what we sow. We have emerged from the struggle of a world built by men and made for men, into one shaped by our own hands. We are a community united in purpose and joy. We raise a new generation not in fear, rivalry, or dread, but in love. Love that grows where anxiety once lived. Love that replaces jealousy with belonging." A murmur of agreement rippled through the gathering.

"Hypsipyle, we also acknowledge the shame of your transgression. While your remorse and repentance are sincere, they are not enough to balance your treachery and sins against the women of Lemnos. We understand this may bring more fear and distress upon you." Hypsipyle did not flinch. "You spared Thoas. In defiance of our covenant, you clung to the father, the symbol of all we rose against. We severed the chain, while you clutched the shackle."

Muffled sobs from the crowd accompanied Alkippe's judgement. "Let the sentence match the crime. You who showed loyalty to the old rule of men shall serve under it. You will live not as one of us, but as what your choice revealed. You are to be sold into slavery. You will be a woman owned. Your body shall carry the burden your heart could not."

Hypsipyle swallowed and breathed deeply, giving the words time to settle. While Alkippe emanated empathy and compassion, her love did not shy away from justice.

"Would you like to respond?" Alkippe offered.

Hypsipyle nodded. She turned to address the women. How beautiful they all were. Many rocked babes in arms and laughed with the fullness of happiness, all blessed by transformation.

She loved them. She looked away, there was so much to say. She coughed and faced them once again.

"The burden laid on me to murder Thoas pressed as heavily as yours. I loved him, as you loved your kin, your husbands, sons, fathers, and brothers. But Thoas ruled as our King. My offense would be judged not as a crime of passion, but treason. This is no excuse."

She paused. The women sat stoic, expressionless. Could they, would they hear her words?

"I am, or was, Queen of Lemnos. Of royal blood. I could not commit an act of treason. So I spared him. I do not know if Dionysus or Poseidon favoured his escape, and I have no recourse to learn the outcome of my action. I mourn his passing as you mourn the loss of your loved ones. We became barren of heart with cruel grief taunting us. This we shared."

She drew a long breath, and aware this would be her last opportunity to speak, she ploughed on, desperate to be understood. "I am a wedge between two loyalties," she began, "My aspirations are yours, that of shared communication, collaboration, respect, spiritual and intuitive goals garnered with passion, emotion, compassion and kindness. We are women, we are sisters.

"Strength and courage are borne from our honesty and desire for truth. I strived to contribute. To nourish my world, our world, with light and wisdom accrued. We are of Earth, the scorch of volcanoes and the consciousness of oceans."

From the crowd, a woman's voice rang out, challenging her. "Guilt traverses your veins. Why choose shame when you could have lived with honour? Who beckoned you?"

Hypsipyle gazed over the faces, seeking the one who spoke. "You misrepresent me. I waged a war between my heart, my soul and my mind. There could never be victory, never be peace.

Shame now dictates my every breath."

A murmur rippled through the gathering.

"But who beckons, you ask? Are you proposing fault lies at the feet of the gods? Am I to blame them for my choices? My predicament? No." She paused. Realisation awakened slow and steady. She recalled the last conversation with her father when he compared her to her mother and she replied that she had grown into something the world made.

"I blame our men. All men. For they are the obstacle denying my truth. Of all I desire. Of all I deserve. Their words control my language, ordains my destiny, and burns my knowledge." Tears began to fall, but Hypsipyle failed to notice.

"Men, tasked by the Mother to be protector, are corrupted by greed, complicit in their grasp for power. But they are forever taunted by an ultimate lack. From jealousy for what they can never achieve. They yearn for the gift we possess. That of true creation. For we are the creators of spirit, of love, founders of peace and joy and pleasure. We are daughters of Crones. We are the Universe for all carried within our wombs."

Her words lifted the energy of the crowd. The women looked around and beheld the babies born, living proof of creating a new Lemnos.

Hypsipyle continued. "Men are frauds and usurpers. They speak lies to hide our past. Misuse their strength in violence. Toward each other, toward us women, toward our children. Believing they are entitled has debased them."

The women nodded in agreement. Without the men, life had been transformed. Hypsipyle drew breath. "It was not some flippant task to murder your menfolk and suffer wounds of torment. It demanded courage and strength. You summoned every speck of integrity, and despite the injury to your soul, remained true to yourself. My disgrace is my compliance. I failed to withstand the pressure imposed from men's tradition with its demands of loyalty and conformity to their ways. Saving my father was an act of treason to myself, and I abhor my cowardice.

"But you offer resolution. I welcome your judgement. Sold into slavery is a fitting punishment. For as long as I uphold the traditions of men, I am enslaved to their invisible fetters. They who disguise their trappings as gifts of comfort and love. Bah, comfort is an illusion."

Hypsipyle wiped the tears with her hands. Overflowing with gratitude she stood proud, claiming her space.

"Comfort entraps the soul." Her voice lowered, the women leaned in. "Once it may have served well. The child needing to escape the fear of trauma creates a space where safety dwells. It becomes familiar, offering refuge. An intimate retreat from the hurt of the world. But residing in this place diminishes the soul's light. Within a sanctuary of habit cushioned by traditions that serve the father, I was dulled. Never broken but eased into a placid distraction that quelled my dreams.

"Safe but stagnant. I sought to retain this security. To live in a cage of certainty. The known, the steadfast. Comfort is a quiet conquest. It asks for nothing, but gives nothing in return. I lost the sharpness of desire. Your judgement is prudent for I am a slave already. I do not fear, nor dread my future. I welcome it. It invokes courage. I am alive again. I am grateful for your wisdom, dear sisters. You have saved me."

*

They roused her from slumber. Caring hands, murmuring voices. Hypsipyle secured her robe and followed the subdued procession.

The humidity of the Hamman greeted her at the top of the steps. She let the robe slip from her shoulders as she descended into the darkened space. The tiles were hot underfoot, heated by the coals of Hephaestus' furnace. Buried deep within the volcano, it simmered and flared, emitting raw bursts of power, maintaining its intense cleansing heat.

Hypsipyle lay upon the marble slab. Its warmth spread through her flesh, and as she sunk into its charm, felt its deepening reach purify her. She sighed into it, her mind slowing to a mumbled bliss. No thought dared interrupt. Sweat swam.

Firm hands, at first tender, began a slow pummelling of her body before extending into a vigorous scrub. Salt crystals were added, exfoliating her skin. The combined pleasure and pain cleansed both body and soul. All tension dissolved from loving touch. Guided to standing, attendants washed her body and anointed the silky softness of her skin with perfumed oils.

Leaving the Haman pertained to a symbolic entering of a new life. Dressed in a simple tunic, Hypsipyle followed the women to the dock. Boats and other seafaring craft lined the harbour. Pollyx held her hand as a measure of love rather than respect. Hypsipyle could expect nothing more, the old woman's gesture corralled her feelings to the base of her throat.

Helios hurried to observe the action and witness a Queen being removed from her throne, reduced to the mortality of common stock. A lone voice wafted on his rays, singing with gentle sorrow. Soon joined by others, all keening their sadness. Cleansed and purified, Hypsipyle allowed tears to fall in solidarity.

LEAVING LEMNOS

Hypsipyle may have appeared calm to the sailors tasked with delivering her to an unknown master, but the further she travelled from the shores of Lemnos, the more her thoughts churned in turmoil. Composure wavered on a precipice of despair in leaving the only home she knew.

If the boat's ambition was to lull her with its sway and soothe her troubled soul, it failed. The elements of wind, water and sun ignored the subtle signs of her vulnerability. The inner sanctity of her pride crumbled and scattered in the windy bluster. Her sense of self eroded with each lick of sea spray. Once strong and carefree, she could no longer recognise who she had become. How could she have got this so wrong? The rhythm of the boat shook up sleeping residue of self-compassion, which disintegrated in the light.

There would be no marble statue honouring her legacy. Chipped away by flawed decisions, she had become a mere plaster cast version of herself. As the journey took her further from home, the splintered wreckage of her past faded with nightfall, and she pondered the price of freedom.

*

A flock of gulls delivered morning. Their bickering and squawking shredded any hope of a peaceful awakening. They followed the boat into the harbour demanding fish guts be spilled over the side. Hypsipyle stood to watch the small fishing village draw close.

Many of the white painted dwellings that lined the shoreline were laced with octopi strung along twine, drying in the morning sun. Cats trolled stone walls searching for tidbits. The port hummed as it moved into preparations for the day.

Hypsipyle sat at the edge of the boat taking her time to disembark into her new life of servitude. Her fingers curled around the rough lip of the railing, as if she were anchoring herself to something known. In this foreign land, every breath told someone else's story.

Staring into the harbour depth, Hypsipyle focussed on her hazy reflection. 'This face used to belong to a Queen who couldn't stop the blood, to a mother who couldn't keep her sons.' The current licked her image like kittens lapping spilt milk.

'Who am I now?'

They will ask her name. It used to matter. It once meant Queen, daughter of King Thoas. She had worn it like a gold brooch, bright with lineage, heavy with meaning. Now, her name echoed the sound of deceit. Of blood dried beneath her feet.

Her face belonged to a stranger. Tribulations etched new lines across her forehead. Her smile thinned into a tight band. This was not the woman who once raised a sceptre. This woman has no kingdom. No home. They will ask her name, but she will not give them her ruin. She tested the silence.

Xene.

It slipped into her ears like silk woven on fate's loom. Subdued. Unnoticed. Stranger. Yes, she is a stranger in this land, but more than that. She is a stranger to the girl who once danced on Lemnian beaches, to the woman who ruled a kingdom and who bore twin sons. She is a stranger to the gods who once answered her prayers.

Xene. A name stripped of lineage, of blood, of expectation. It was both armour and confession. It tasted of anonymity. Xene. The stranger. But also the one who endured. She rolled the name around her mouth. It was not a lie, just not the whole truth. A name to keep her safe. Let them ask. She would answer.

EURYDICE

67

"Who is that?" Queen Eurydice had never attended the slave market, but newly married, she wished to secure a trusted nursemaid in hope of prompting the gods to bless her marriage bed. She did not trust Lycurgus' opinion on such maternal matters, and wanted to assess any potential servant for such precious duty. Eager to please his new bride, King Lycurgus agreed for her to accompany him to this arena of flesh and woeful tidings. While not a place befitting a Queen, he had already surmised his wife was comprised of contradictions. Seductive and sharp, her tenderness cloaked in thorns. He had married well.

Her attendant approached the Slave Master with her enquires and returned with information and gossip. She wondered which to tell her Mistress first. "It is rumoured the woman is of royal heritage. Her name is Xene. She is from Lemnos, sold into slavery through the misconduct of betrayal. She neither denies nor confirms her past."

Eurydice appraised the tall stately woman. Hypsipyle returned her gaze, before remembering to lower her eyes. Hypsipyle frowned, annoyed for not having yet learned to humble herself as her new status demanded.

"She has armour in her veins and secrets in her blood," Eurydice deduced, and turned to her husband. "I wish to speak with that woman."

The Slave Master led Hypsipyle to the royal couple. She bowed her head and did not raise it even when addressed. She repeated a silent mantra. 'I am a slave. I have no rights. Even my dignity can be bought.'

"You are from Lemnos?" enquired the Queen. The question should have been expected but the mention of home sent a dagger through her heart. Hypsipyle pinched herself to distract her thoughts. "Yes, your majesty." Her dialect would have exposed any lie.

"Who sold you into slavery, or were you born a slave?"

"I am a prize of war," Hypsipyle answered. She did not want to lie to the Queen. Ambiguity obliged. She could never confess of her wrongdoing, but spoke as close to the truth as she dared. "Loyalty to my father created the circumstances I find myself in. The women of Lemnos are honourable and fair-minded, and I am grateful for their justice."

Her answer puzzled Eurydice. Many royal women became trophies through men's battle conquests, but not acquainted with the history of Lemnos to further query Hypsipyle's response, she misinterpreted her guilt as grief.

"I am seeking a nursemaid."

"I have birthed twins, but they were taken from me. I possess a mother's love that has nowhere to go."

The Queen turned to Lycurgus. "I have chosen," she informed him. "This woman will do well for us."

EURYDICE'S FRIENDSHIP

Eurydice invited Hypsipyle to join her in the shade of the plane tree's embrace. Its gnarled trunk carried centuries of whispered confidences as its overreaching broad leaves provided respite from Helios' sting. Enticed by its promise of coolness, Eurydice reclined on a day bed, swollen with child.

Although Hypsipyle had been at the palace for a cycle of returning seasons, she remained an enigma. A nursemaid, but somewhat more. Eurydice had forgiven Hypsipyle's lack of domestic skills, reminding herself she wanted a nurse for her baby, not an attendant. But her aloofness was cause for concern. 'Perhaps this is the way of Lemnian women,' Eurydice thought, unable to penetrate her defences. With the imminent birth of her baby, Eurydice set out to discover why Hypsipyle chose to keep to herself.

Hypsipyle appreciated Eurydice's kind and respectful treatment of her staff, and held her in high regard. But while she took pleasure in Eurydice's company, being alone with her heightened her fear of exposure. Her cautious friendship with the young Queen necessitated an attentive focus. The need to conceal her deceit consumed her energy.

"You betrayed?" Eurydice's unexpected question bit hard. Hypsipyle jolted. Her pulse quickened as alarm chased the blood through her veins. Eurydice's conversation, her humour, and sharp intelligence felt dangerous. Fate paused.

"Betrayed?" Hypsipyle repeated. Thoughts tumbled, but none supplied an answer to speak out aloud. Her inner monologue panicked at the Queen's blunt inquiry. 'Why would the Queen ask this now? Did she know something?'

"At the slave market, the Slave Master told my attendant that your crime was a transgression of dishonesty." Eurydice waited, giving Hypsipyle time to respond.

Hypsipyle fumbled. Answers clogged her throat. Belief in managing to hold the past at bay exposed itself as a delusion. All assumptions withered. Her mind stumbled into a maze of confusion, and she reached for deflection to steady her. Incessant questions bombarded her with options: 'Why do you want to know? Why now? Are you going to sell me? Have I not proved trustworthy? Can we not leave the past to sleep?' She replied with the only words that found her tongue. "Why do you ask?"

Eurydice watched Hypsipyle deliberate. Her observation was subtle, for she fussed with cushions, drank from her cup of cool-minted tea, stroked her stomach, and picked a flower, twirling it between her fingers. She was a master of dalliance.

Hypsipyle struggled. Exhaustion and fear controlled her tongue. Nothing further could be said. She hung her head.

Eurydice pursued her. "Betrayal is a learned behaviour," she said. "To break an oath you need an example to follow. Who betrayed you?"

Hypsipyle reeled. "Who betrayed me?"

"Or perhaps, dear Xene, my question should be, where lies your anger?"

"I am not angry," snapped Hypsipyle. Even to her own ears her tone sounded like a rebuke. She softened in apology, "Your majesty."

"Eurydice is fine," the Queen replied. "I hope we are friends. I am not afraid of familiarity between us. After all you will be responsible for my most precious treasure." She rubbed her belly for emphasis.

A sense of urgency surged through Hypsipyle. The desire to run, to flee, screamed at her. Eurydice's pregnancy presented a diversion. "Can I get you anything? Are you comfortable?" Eurydice was not to be played.

"So perhaps your grief has not yet transpired to anger?" Eurydice suggested. "Disbelief, denial, guilt, sadness and regret, leading up to the unfairness of it all." Gentleness interwove the conversation with compassion. The Queen rephrased her question. "Xene, where lies your sorrow?"

"Everywhere," Hypsipyle replied, defeated. She looked at Eurydice. Into warm chestnut eyes expressing concern. She plunged into them, spiralling into unfamiliar depths where care and tenderness enveloped her. It was unknown terrain.

A small fissure ruptured. Her mother died when she was too young to understand but old enough to remember her smell, her laugh and her love. While Pollyx had been benevolent, she was busy managing the palace. Even her beloved father, lost and bereaved, sailed off on raiding parties. Sometimes he returned with strange women, but they never stayed long, and Hypsipyle learned not to get close, not to share her broken heart with anyone.

Complexity scourged Hypsipyle's face. The crack within widened as agony ripped through her. The warmth of Eurydice's skin taking her hand unleashed inner daemons. "My mother died," she stammered. The force of a lifetime of silence and constraint proved too great. Her admission erupted into heaving sobs.

Eurydice did not let go of her hand. She did not speak.

"But death," Hypsipyle wiped her face, "is not betrayal."

Eurydice's gentle response held firm. "She left you. You were a child and your mother went away without you."

Any pretence of decorum collapsed. Years of repression cracked open and Hypsipyle succumbed to the chaos. Her raw cries were as though the gods themselves wailed through her. She clung to Eurydice's hand, a steady anchor against the turbulence, as memories rose to torment her with the loss of love and sadness she endured. Until anger emerged. Its rage shoved aside the delicate fragility of passive submission and unfurled its assault with a ferocity that sent spasms through her body. In the midst of its frenzied rampage, the voice of a vulnerable child screamed from within. "Why?" she called out, "Why did you leave me?" The storm shook her body with a violent furore, until finally, the small, abandoned child curled up into herself and wept. Then slept.

Darkness descended with a gentle caress. Hypsipyle awoke. A blanket had been placed over her and lit torches danced in the shadows. Eurydice gave a little snore before she too awoke. She smiled at Hypsipyle. A mother's smile or, perhaps, a friend's.

In the dim light of evening when the veil between day and night interweave, Hypsipyle acknowledged feeling different. Something diffused or shifted. A sense of lightness, a feeling of being somewhat free replaced her harsh companion of restraint. She looked with gratitude at the very pregnant woman silhouetted by flamed light.

"My name is Hypsipyle," she confessed.

"Hypsipyle." Eurydice spoke her name. "But you live here now, and I shall call you by the name you call yourself, Xene."

OPHELTES

73

Hypsipyle held him to her breast. He had already outgrown his newborn scent but she relished the smell of his innocence. The power of unconditional love channelled through every cell, eclipsing the love for her father, where love and loyalty blinded her, her love for Jason borne of passion and lust, and even the short burst of love for her sons, torn from her breast.

Her heart, hardened by life, melted into his softness and the grasp of his tiny hand on her finger. She cooed and rocked him. Her arms tingled with the texture of trust. She had forgotten its depth. She breathed in life and hope and new beginnings. His life and hers reclaimed. "Opheltes," she purred. Saviour to her soul, offering peace, offering grace. She floated.

SEVEN AGAINST THEBES

Helios smouldered with impatience and scorched his path across the sky in frustration. Bored by mortal events panning out below, he took leave behind a passing cloud to snooze. The shadow spanned across a dusty plain as seven travellers crested a hill, their cloaks stiff from their journey's grime and with tempers short from thirst. Leading the small band of men rode Adrastus, king of Argos. He slowed as he approached a grove of cypress trees marking the outskirts of Nemea, and spied Hypsipyle carrying a young child in her arms.

Hypsipyle shifted Opheltes onto her hip and watched the strangers approach. Adrastus signalled to halt. He dismounted, and navigated the scratch of his voice into a diplomatic tone. "Madam, we seek water and shade."

"This is sacred ground. The grove belongs to Zeus," Hypsipyle replied.

"We mean no harm. I am Adrastus of Argos, son of Talaus. These are my companions. We are warriors bound for Thebes, to lay rightful claim to the throne denied to my son-in-law, Polynices."

Argos. Hypsipyle's heart quaked at the echo of this land. She frowned. "You march against Thebes?"

"Yes," Adrastus said. "Seven leaders, seven gates. Justice demands it, and blood shall answer blood."

Her attention turned to the child, small, restless in the heat. "This is Opheltes," she said. "Son of King Lycurgus and Queen Eurydice. I am his nurse."

A slight commotion behind Adrastus interrupted them. One of the men spoke up. "Adrastus, I believe we should continue on."

"Ah, dear brother," Adrastus turned to his brother-in-law, Amphiaraus. "Another prophesy? Shall we die of thirst before entering the gates of Thebes?" Amphiaraus shook his head and grumbled into his beard. He was a reluctant participant in this expedition, having foreseen the campaign was doomed. But his wife Eriphyle, sister to Adrastus betrayed him for the necklace of the Goddess Harmonia and, having been given the power to settle disputes between her husband and brother, ordered him to join the war. Adrastus turned back to Hypsipyle.

"The child seems restless," he said, offering a weary smile. "As are we all."

Hypsipyle's eyes flicked toward the grove. "There is a spring, not far. Let me show you. But make haste before the Queen returns."

The men followed as Hypsipyle led them down a narrow path. At the spring, they fell to their knees and drank deeply. "It is good of you," Adrastus said between gulps, "to show mercy to strangers." Satisfied, they then filled their water bags. Hypsipyle watched them, her own lips dry.

She set Opheltes down upon a bed of wild celery and knelt beside Adrastus to quench her own thirst. "I know what it is to lose a kingdom," she replied.

Adrastus paused, captive to curiosity. Hypsipyle filled a small container and returned to Opheltes. Her scream pierced the hot still valley. The men leapt to their feet as Hypsipyle's knees buckled and she crumpled to the ground.

Opheltes had rolled onto the dirt, and a telltale glisten of a svelte scaled skin signalled a fleeing snake. Adrastus unsheathed his sword and sliced the serpent in two. The grove fell into dismayed silence.

Opheltes lay dead, the serpent's strike swift and cruel. Hypsipyle knelt beside him, stricken, shaking her head in denial of the horror she faced. Adrastus stood grim, his sword slick with the snake's blood.

The child's lifeless body was soft, floppy. The tragedy did not deny his beauty, shrouded in an ephemeral tranquillity. Such translucent serenity belied Hypsipyle's mounting shock and disbelief. She closed his eyes with a tender touch and kissed his tiny forehead. Even without his life spark he suffused love. She sagged, comprehension registering the full meaning of his listless form. She clung to him in desperation as another piecing howl fractured the silence. Grief claimed her as its prize. Her throat snagged. She dared not speak lest her tears never cease.

Grief doesn't frolic. It doesn't beckon, tempt or entice. It doesn't sneak up, or cuddle or whisper sweet nothings. It is raw and brutal and violent. It strikes its target with a bolt of devastation, destroying happiness, obliterating joy. Her defences down, Hypsipyle rocked, lamenting the treasure clutched to her breast. Life was a mockery.

She felt strong arms raise her. Amphiaraus helped her to her feet as Eurydice, having heard the screams, came running. The wind loves nothing more than to spread the news of tragedy. Eurydice stopped. Abrupt. The fear in her eyes begged for refutal.

Hypsipyle wobbled, fragile with anguish. Misery shrivelled her face into a scrunched ball, her eyes never leaving her nightmare. She became aware of someone intruding in her desolation. Too close. She looked up. Eurydice. The sight of her friend sent a shuddering release and a deluge of tears drowned her vision. Slow and heavy, Hypsipyle held out the burden of grief. Her gesture awakened Eurydice from her trance and she snatched Opheltes and buried her face into his swaddling.

The clatter of hooves signalled the King's arrival and shattered the tense shock holding everyone captive. Lycurgus dismounted, his face darkened as he surveyed the scene. His distressed wife, Hypsipyle weeping, and the Seven standing in solemn witness. Bewilderment fuelled his judgement. "You." He bellowed, and strode toward Hypsipyle. "You were charged with his care."

She bowed her head. There were no words of comfort for him.

"You left him. On the ground..." The Oracle warned. Opheltes was not to be put on the ground until he learned to walk.

"Not on the ground, no." Hypsipyle stammered.

Adrastus stepped forward. "King Lycurgus, if I may speak."

The King clenched his fists. "This is not your affair, stranger."

"With respect, it is," Adrastus said. "We are a party to this tragedy. We asked her for aid, and she consented, not knowing the cost. The gods, it seems, had a darker plan."

Lycurgus held his fury and said nothing.

Adrastus stepped closer. "Let his death not be a beginning of vengeance, but of remembrance. Let it not end in more sorrow, but mark the start of something greater."

Lycurgus growled. "Speak plainly."

"Let us honour Opheltes. Declare games in his name. Funeral rites in the form of a sacred contest. Call them the Nemean Games and let men contend not for gold, but for glory and the memory of a lost child. Let his name echo through the generations, not in grief, but in greatness."

The other six warriors nodded their assent.

The King looked from Adrastus to his wife clutching his son. He spoke, his voice low. "You propose a noble tribute. What of retribution?"

"The nurse did not kill your son," Adrastus said. "A beast

of the gods did. But in her kindness to strangers, she sealed a tragedy she never intended. Mercy would honour your son more than blood."

Lycurgus knelt to help Eurydice to her feet. As they left the grove, he turned, "Let it be done."

*

In the days that followed, word spread of the inaugural Nemean Games to honour the death of the King's son, now called Archemorus, the Forerunner of Doom. Restricted to warriors and their sons to underscore the festival's solemn and funeral-like tone, challengers came from far and wide to compete for glory.

THE NEMEAN GAMES

The day of the funeral games was declared a day of honour. To Hypsipyle, it rang hollow. They named it honour, yet through contests of strength, speed, and endurance, she heard only the thunder of pride in a celebration of men's prowess. Where in their contests lay the ache of love and memory, the cries of the women who had lost? This so-called honour excluded those bearing the deepest wound. She felt the injustice to her core.

Life's wisdom taught her that mourning was not a spectacle but a sacred weaving of love and loss, a binding thread between the living and the dead. But here, women's emotional connection through ritual mourning held no place. Usurped by men's sport, respect for the dead privileged public display over intimacy, and bound public expression of honour to men's ideals. Men claimed the right to define remembrance on their own terms. Opheltes was not only lost, but his memory stolen and reshaped as triumph for them. Women's pain bled, hidden behind closed doors, condemned as chaos, and silenced beneath the roar of a crowd. She grieved for Eurydice.

The image of the young Queen pierced her heart. They had not spoken since the tragedy. Eurydice avoided her, denying her access to pay respects to Opheltes lying in state. Hypsipyle bore her haunting guilt in solitude, and in the quiet of the empty nursery, she prayed to the Moirai, the three sisters weaving her destiny, to either cut her life-thread or condemn her to a deserving future. Whichever the worse.

Lycurgus had ordered her from the palace once the Games

were finished. Her exiled freedom tasted bitter, but she refused to coddle any fear from his decree. Once more she would learn to adapt, all the while paying reverence to her despair as an altar to kneel before.

Illusion had peeled away, and she accepted whatever the gods ordained. She had failed their test of love, and now love mocked her. It stole her father, Jason, her babies and Opheltes. The giddiness in her head tormented her, but at least it provided distraction from the heavy numbness swallowing her entire being. Fatigue clung as a constant companion.

Leaving the nursery, Hypsipyle made her way through the empty walkways of the palace toward the arena. The cheers of the crowd echoed through the corridors as the Nemean Games reached their climax. She quickened her pace. She must attend despite the shackles of grief.

Among the competitors, two young men, identical in build and bearing were preparing for the final event of the day. Thoas rolled his shoulders and flexed his fingers, the muscles in his legs twitched with anticipation. Beside him, his twin brother Euneus stretched with calm precision. Traveling the distance to offer condolence was fuelled by their love of competitive sport.

"I am much improved brother. This time the race will be mine." Thoas boasted, eager to win. "There will be a first time, but it will be once, if at all," Euneus replied. "But not today."

At the blast of a horn, the two young men joined other runners at the starting line. Digging their toes into the packed earth, they gave each other a quick nod. While always competitors, their rivalry was born from affection.

They sprang forward, feet pounding the earth, arms pumping in rhythm. A dozen young men raced, but the contest narrowed between the two. As they ploughed ahead of the field, step for step they matched each other. The crowd cheered their fierce, synchronised style.

As they crossed the finish line together, Adrastus, cloaked in black robes of mourning and adjudicating the race, hesitated. Neither brother clearly won. Attendants approached them and, upon learning who was the elder of the twins, Adrastus proclaimed, "The winner of the final footrace is Euneus, first born son of Jason of the Argonauts." The crowd erupted, roaring in adoration.

As Adrastus placed a wreath of wild celery representing the transitory nature of life, upon Euneus' head, he spoke. "I knew your father. He was a hero to many." Euneus smiled with polite acknowledgement. His father was also known to many for his treacherous behaviour resulting in the murder of his younger step-brothers, children of Medea.

Hypsipyle edged closer to the podium. Watching from the fringes, her hands trembled. 'It cannot be.' Disbelief toyed with her emotions. She watched Euneus receive his crown as adulation from the stand filled the arena. The way he moved, the familiar curve of his smile, the thick golden locks of hair. She searched the faces of the other participants and saw his identical brother. "Jason," she whispered, "are these our sons?"

Her question caught the wind's attention, which shimmied toward the podium and passed over Euneus like a breath from the past. Euneus turned and caught Hypsipyle's startled gaze. At the same time, a young maiden offered him a bouquet, and in that moment of distraction, Hypsipyle fled. When Euneus looked back, she had vanished.

"Did you see that woman?" he asked Thoas. "Near the judges' platform?" Euneus couldn't shake her image, or hearing her name carried on the wind.

Thoas shrugged. "There were dozens."

"She was watching us... our eyes met."

"Sounds like you've had too much sun." Thoas joked. "Come, let us celebrate. We have earned this victory."

*

Helios wearied of the day's commemoration and dipped below the horizon. From the shadows, Hypsipyle observed the twins, savouring vague memories of the little time she nursed them. To see them as young men felt like a gift from the gods. She retreated into a quiet olive grove behind the temple precinct where the air was cool and fragrant with thyme. She sat content, reflecting in a soothing peace.

"Hypsipyle?"

She startled on hearing her name. It had not been spoken since her confession to Eurydice in the garden, many seasons ago. She took refuge in her shawl, covering her head, hoping to arrive at an answer. Should she deny and maintain her lie? Did it matter anymore? She had already lost everything. She stood to see Adrastus approach. She straightened her back, firm with resolve. "Yes," she confirmed.

"The Queen spoke your name. Now I understand your comment about losing your kingdom. You have been thought long dead."

"That woman is. I am no longer Queen, but a nursemaid, and not good at that either." She fought back a wave of pressure behind her eyes.

"Do your sons know you?"

His words sliced through her. Hypsipyle couldn't speak. She trembled, engulfed in suffering. Wretchedness entrapped her. Every breath infused distress. She swallowed, looked away, then looked back at Adrastus. Her eyes filled with tears she refused to shed.

Adrastus stepped forward and took her into his arms. He held her shaking body. His compassion ignored the last traces of her stoicism, and his kindness paved the way for her tears to fall. She wept into his chest. When the intensity of her sobs lessened, Hypsipyle pulled away, bestowing Adrastus a small, embarrassed smile of thanks.

"Stay here, Hypsipyle. Wait for me. I will return," he said.

She sat and wiped her face. Her story known, the air around her shifted. Disclosure contained an offering of release, a hint of courage and the slight flavour of healing. If the gods decreed she was to leave this earthly plane, she would not fear, for she had faced her purgatory.

Adrastus returned with Euneus and Thoas. "Good night Hypsipyle, may peace be your constant companion." He slipped away before she could reply. The two young men stared, speechless by his words. Euneus nodded, recognising her as the woman near the podium. He espied a regal air that defied the worn fabric of her robes.

She drew her veil back with quivering fingers and looked up at them. "Forgive me," Hypsipyle said, her voice breaking the stillness. "You are sons of Jason?"

The young men spoke together. "You are Hypsipyle? Our mother?" The truth loomed, too big to comprehend. Questions imploded, stealing their voice. Euneus rubbed the hem of the deep purple cloak draped over his shoulders at the mention of his father. Jason had bequeathed it to him. It offered a way through the tangled mess of raw emotion. "You presented this to him," he stated.

"It belonged to your grandfather." She turned to Thoas, "Your namesake. It was a gift from your great-grandfather Dionysus. I entrusted it to Jason when he left." Desperate for word about her lover, she bit back her curiosity, allowing her beloved sons to satiate their own need for knowledge. Later she would learn Jason died an ignoble death when struck by a rotting piece of timber from the Argo. Ironic that the symbol of his heroism became his coffin. A poetic end, some would say.

Thoas studied his mother before him. Her eyes, her voice, bereavement imprinted in her skin. "We were told you died. Or disappeared. Father never said much, just that Lemnos belonged to the past."

"And yet here you are," Euneus added. "After all this time. Why didn't you find us?"

Fresh tears slid down Hypsipyle's cheeks. "Your father promised to return." She could see Jason's face in the structure of their cheekbones, the lushness of their lips. "In Lemnos I betrayed my sisters. I was not fit to be their Queen. For punishment, I was sold into slavery. Queen Eurydice recognised my royal heritage, and I became nursemaid to a child fated to die."

Hypsipyle paused, sensitive to the swirl of feelings evoked from speaking of her friendship. Once treasured, now destroyed. And yet Eurydice spoke to Adrastus. A flourish of love pulsed. She looked up at Euneus and Thoas. Her dearest friend, who mourned the loss of her child, had given her back her sons. "I lost everything. Until today."

The grove leaned in, edging closer to the verge of a story. The wind rustled the branches with anticipation. "I think we should sit," suggested Euneus. They found a rock beneath an ancient tree, and as dusk slipped over Nemea, Hypsipyle prepared to tell them everything. Of Lemnos, of exile, of a life endured in shame.

Euneus, draped in the regal cloak of his grandfather Thoas, returned to Lemnos and claimed his birthright. Historians and poets went on to credit him with purifying the island of its blood-guilt by extinguishing all hearth fires for nine days before relighting them with sacred flame from Apollo's altar at Delos.

Hypsipyle's courage lived on in her son, Euneus. He provisioned the Greek fleet on its way to Troy and ransomed a Trojan prisoner with a silver urn offered to King Thoas by Phoenician traders. Her life, once shadowed by fear and secrecy, lives on in the memory of Lemnos, carried in the songs of the Euneidae, cithara musicians who honour a woman's love, her courage, and the strength to face the weight of consequence.

Simone de Beauvoir coined the term *'absolute truth'* to expose how the male perspective is perceived as the default. Writing through a feminist lens refuses to play this game – to sideline women's stories and experiences. Why perpetuate a point of view that negates women's lived experience, history, and knowledge?

Women are not a deviation to standard (male) humanity but, because history defers to a white male perspective, women are positioned as a minority. In framing women in this niche identity, we are set up to be forgettable, or, as Caroline Criado Perez writes in *The Invisible Woman*, "Dispensable – from culture, from history, from data ... women become invisible" (2020, 24).

Hypsipyle's story is one of the most infamous events in Greek mythology. The 'Lemnian Crime' is an act that came to symbolise the ultimate punishment for infidelity and neglect. It is a story muddied by the complexities of loyalty and sacrifice. Saving her father is lauded as an act of compassion, but it comes at a great personal cost. Ultimately Hypsipyle's action is a betrayal of the people she governs, which leads to her downfall.

Within a traditional, patriarchal framework, Hypsipyle is exalted as a virtuous daughter. Her loyalty, filial piety, and obedience to paternal bonds are upheld as noble traits. Risking her life to save her father, King Thoas, demonstrates her expected deference to male authority, even when it defies collective female action. Her compassion is celebrated not as agency, but as self-sacrificial virtue aligned with the ideal of a 'good woman'.

A feminist reading casts Hypsipyle's act as a betrayal of solidarity. In choosing to protect her father, she undermines the collective uprising shared by the Lemnian women. Her decision is more than personal, it is political. As Queen, she betrays those she leads, prioritising patriarchal loyalty over female autonomy. She compromises her own safety and position, which suggests an internalised obligation to male authority that undermines her sovereignty and self-respect.

Hypsipyle's agency and the impact of the emotional toll as a consequence of her deceit is largely absent from the existing fragments of texts written by a long list of ancient (male) Greek poets and historians. These narratives fail to reveal or explain the intimate burden Hypsipyle bore. They also lack any unanimous confirmation how the women of Lemnos discovered Hypsipyle's lies. They do, however, acknowledge Hypsipyle was an honourable, intelligent and courageous woman.

I took creative liberty to write an account highlighting her struggle with her conscience and her integrity in choosing resolution. In *Hypsipyle and the Curse of Lemnos*, Hypsipyle accepts responsibility for her choices, and displays courage in taking accountability for her actions. My interpretation seeks to offer a more visceral interpretation of her ordeal.

This novella sits comfortably on the shelf with its precursors of *The Women Unveiled* series, as well the works of other notable authors who retell the myths and histories of women. Recounting these stories is a call to action, a call for change. In extracting our narratives from the shadows, women become seen and heard. We owe this to our daughters.

Ancient Greek poets and historians who wrote about Hypsipyle include:

Apollonius of Rhodes, (circa 3rd C) *Argonautica*
Euripides (circa 410 BC) *Hypsipyle*
Apollodorus, (c 1st or 2nd C) *Bibliotheca*
Gaius Julius Hyginus, *Fabulae*
Ovid, *Heroides*
Valerius Flaccus, (circa 1st C) *Argonautica*
Aeschylus (458 BC) *The Libation Bearers*
Sophocles, (c 400 BC) *Lemniai*
Pinder, *Pythian*
Herodotus (circa 5th BC)
Publius Papinius Statius (1st C) *Thebaid*
Homer, (c 850 – 700 BC) *Iliad*

ACKNOWLEDGEMENTS

Hypsipyle and the Curse of Lemnos found its voice and rhythm through the creative and immersive workshops run by author Jan Cornall in Ischia, Italy. Thank you Jan, for your inspired exploration of a writing journey through the senses and connection to the elements.

And much gratitude to the wonderful writers and authors who participated and shared my journey: Antonietta, Robin, Annie, Dan, Caroline, Don, Jemana and Lyn. Reading the raw versions of emerging work was often challenging, but it was always met with your kindness, generosity and support.

It was an act of courage for me to sign up to these workshops on offer by The Creative Escape. Fortune favours the brave. Big thanks for this adventure to Jen Richardson and Luisa Donati.

My support team of Jane Ormond and Dom Bongiovanni continue to offer honest and wise advice and suggestions. I appreciate being able to reach out, and your care and critique for my work is greatly valued. Many thanks.

Other books from the author
Fiction
Dancing the Labyrinth
Delphi
The Bringer of Happiness

Non-fiction
The Little Book of Red Flags
The Little Book of Apologies

Dancing the Labyrinth

I think this is the kind of book that finds you where you are at.
So, if finds you, answer its call. **Ioana, Amazon**

Martin's dreamy, esoteric book of female empowerment,
maternal love, and overcoming abuse is dark, breathtaking,
painful, and lovely, all at once. **Booklife / Publisher Weekly**

Dancing the Labyrinth is strange, beautiful, and riddled with
pain and growth. The blending of past and present, myth and
reality, feeling and concrete experience, makes for a highly
unique read. **BookLife / Publisher Weekly**

Dancing the Labyrinth brings the inequalities and injustices that
women have faced through the centuries to the forefront
and gives a message of tranquility, unity, and the collective
efforts required for a positive change in society. **Jane Riley,
The Book Commentary**

This novel is sure to open minds to past, present, and future
understanding of acceptance and healing, while imploring

exploration into ancient and current meanings of femininity and belonging. ***Booklife / Publisher Weekly***

Karen Martin ... creates a protagonist that readers will love; she is genuinely flawed, resilient, and an embodiment of the frustrations and pains that most women have carried with them over centuries. ***The Book Commentary***

Like a painting, Martin did a wonderful job at weaving the stories and characters together, never losing the thread. ***Hannah Barry, Goodreads***

Karen Martin attempted something risky and extremely difficult, but at the same time rare: ***Makis Petsas, (Chania, Crete)***

Martin's message of female solidarity and the possibility of changing not events in the past, but how we feel and respond to them in the present is a positive one ***Elaine Graham-Leigh, Reedsy***

The sensually imagined matriarchal community life which Karen Martin describes in *Dancing the Labyrinth* is phenomenal. ***Tamara Tovey, Amazon***

The Bringer of Happiness

A beautiful evocative remembrance for the soul. A multi-sensory story that sweeps through time and reverses the spirals of realties and offer the reader a chance to return to the knowingness of the soul. ***Anne Marie, Goodreads***

In the vividly realized historical novel that follows, playwright/ author Martin continues the striking storytelling of *Dancing in the Labyrinth*, exploring stories of women in history and myth pushing against the boundaries of patriarchal societies. ***BookLife / Publisher Weekly***

Martin's prose is beautifully descriptive and immersive, drawing you into the sights, sounds and smells of the various stops along the way. The underlying factual aspects make for a really interesting backdrop. ***James Browne, Goodreads***

For those lovers of the television series 'Quantum Leap,' this is a must read. ***Kelly McDonough, Goodreads***

The mythologies and fictionalized story create a unique and powerful narrative ... a must-read for anyone interested in exploring new perspectives on religion and spirituality. ***Manish Gaur, Goodreads***

Currently, where everything can end up being controversial, especially regarding religion, Karen's book is courageous and revolutionary. ***Manik & Sayee, favbookshelf***

The Bringer of Happiness is a fascinating story that blends Fantasy, Greek Mythology, Paganism, Spirituality and Religion together to produce a truly enlightening and thought-provoking tale. ***The Book Dragon***

A narrative of historical events, themes of personal growth, destiny, faith, and the power of religion explore Sara and her mother's story. ***DocMonster, Amazon***

Delphi

Delphi is a celebration of myth and self-discovery, offering a rewarding experience filled with beauty, complexity, and wonder. **Literary Titan**

Delphi is undeniably a unique and magical book. Its lush and engaging characters, along with its intricate tapestry of myths and legends, paint a world that fantasy enthusiasts will find hard to resist. **Literary Titan**

The narrative in *Delphi* is full of feminine power. **Philip Chrysopoulos, Greek Reporter**

A thoughtful and insightful novel that invites the reader to dip into the Castalia spring and converse with the Oracle within. **Dina Gerolymou, SBS RADIO**

At its heart, *Delphi* is an invigorating story about motherhood, nurturing, and protection. **Kent Lane, Indie Reader**

Like the place and the myths surrounding it, *Delphi* is a sophisticated, nuanced and often disconcerting exploration of trauma and how this manifests itself within a quest for self-identity. **Dean Kalimniou, Neos Kosmos**

Don't miss this follow up to the Eyelands Book Award Winner, **Dancing the Labyrinth.** Spectacular reading. **Book Commentary**

The blending of past and present, myth and reality, feeling and concrete experience, makes for a highly unique read. ***Booklife/ Publisher Weekly***

Excellent story! Totally engrossing! Looking forward to reading more by this author! Could not put this down! ***Netgalley***

ABOUT THE AUTHOR

Karen Martin is an award-winning playwright and author. She ran away with the circus, created plays in prisons, and strived to create transformational theatre experiences.

She received a Local History Award and the Ewa Czajor Memorial Award for *The Women's Jail Project*.

Her debut novel *Dancing the Labyrinth* won the Eyelands Book Award 2024. The Greek translation is published by Radamanthys Publications. Her second novel *The Bringer of Happiness* was inspired from Languedoc folklore. *Delphi*, the sequel to *Dancing the Labyrinth*, received a Silver Literary Titan Award, and can be read as a stand-alone novel.

Karen's non-fiction includes *The Little Book of Red Flags* and *The Little Book of Apologies*. This series of Little Books take on a humorous approach to relationships.

Please review

Word of mouth is important to independent authors. If you enjoyed this novella, please leave a rating and/or review on the site where purchased, or Goodreads. This helps spread the word.

Requesting your local library to order it also provides support.

Subscribe for updates: https://www.kazjoypress.com/contact

How to reach the author:

https://www.kazjoypress.com

- I am happy to come and chat at your book club or event either in person or via ZOOM
- Please sign up to my mailing list via my website

Also by Karen Martin

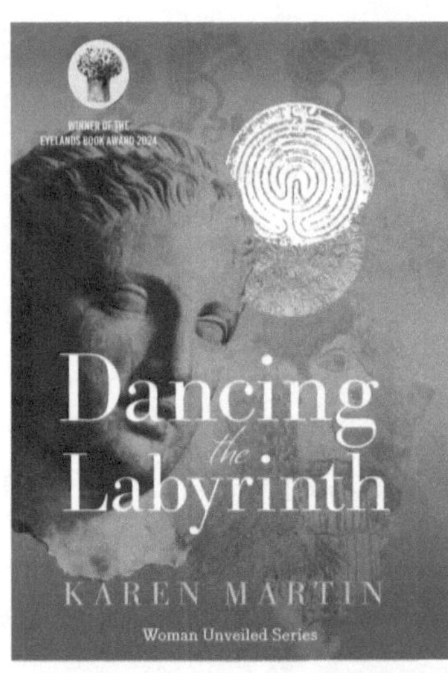